The fleeing man sped toward the parked cars.

Drawing closer to his quarry, Michael launched himself forward and grabbed for the man's feet. He succeeded in wrapping an arm around his knees and the two of them went down in a sprawl. Just before they hit the ground, Michael heard a sudden, harsh crack.

He knew immediately something was wrong. The man fell too loosely. Normally a person would tighten up a little, even if he'd been trained professionally to fall.

Rolling to his feet, Michael kept one hand locked around the man's ankle so he wouldn't get away. One glance assured Michael that wouldn't be the case.

A trickle of blood slid down his attacker's cheek and dripped off his nose from a round wound on his temple.

D0036687

Cast of Characters

Michael and Molly Graham—The young couple have come to Blackpool for a simpler life... only things in the small town are anything but simple.

DCI Paddington—The stolid inspector has a laid-back approach to investigation—so laid-back that it's fuelled rumors he's only in Blackpool to bide his time until retirement.

The Crowes—The members of the Crowe family are reputed to have more secrets than they have money. And they keep both very well. Especially those of their most notorious ancestor, Charles Crowe....

Rohan Wallace—Michael's friend clings to life in the hospital, shot by Aleister Crowe for trespassing on his land. But what was he doing there? What was so important that Rohan would risk his very life?

Stefan Draghici—The head of the gypsy clan that has come to Blackpool to reclaim the fortune in gold they say was stolen from their ancestors by Charles Crowe. Their search for the gold has come up empty, however, and the Draghicis are becoming desperate....

Lockwood Nightingale—Aleister's devoted attorney. How far will he go to protect his client's interests—and his own?

Greed, jealousy, betrayal, trickery, murder—secrets are the heart of Blackpool.

MYSTERY CASE FILES

Unearthed

A BLACKPOOL MYSTERY

Jordan Gray

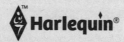

Harlequin®

TORONTO NEW YORK LONDON
AMSTERDAM PARIS SYDNEY HAMBURG
STOCKHOLM ATHENS TOKYO MILAN MADRID
PRAGUE WARSAW BUDAPEST AUCKLAND

Special thanks and acknowledgment to Mel Odom for his contribution to this work.

Recycling programs
for this product may
not exist in your area.

ISBN-13: 978-0-373-83754-0

UNEARTHED

CHAPTER ONE

HOW CLOSE COULD A MAN COME TO death before he gave up the fight and slid into that dark abyss? Michael Graham stared down at the still, unresponsive figure in the white field of the hospital bed. He didn't know how many times the question had filled his mind during the past five days.

"He hasn't quit fighting." The middle-aged nurse jotted notes on the clipboard she held. She didn't look at Michael but he knew she had sized him up as closely as she had the patient. "That's a good sign. You have to take hope in that, Mr. Graham."

"I know. I do take hope in that, Mrs. Guilder. Thank you." Michael leaned against the wall near the room's slatted window. Merciful Angels Hospital conducted business within an old building in Blackpool, but the interior had been gutted and refitted with modern equipment and dutiful personnel like Nurse Guilder.

The woman shot Michael a measuring glance. "Have you been taking care of yourself?"

"I have." Michael lied easily, but he had the suspicion that the nurse instantly saw through him.

"Sometimes the sickness of a friend is hardest on those around them. At least the people in the hospital are getting rest and being monitored. You might try getting a little more sleep."

Michael couldn't argue. He felt bone-tired and twitchy, the way he did in the final stages of putting a video-game project together, almost ready to go gold and turn a new game loose on the public. Those times had always been particularly draining. But they'd been nothing like watching over Rohan Wallace these past five days since he'd been shot by Aleister Crowe, who claimed Rohan had been trespassing on his property. Michael blamed himself for the near-death of his friend. Hadn't he dragged him into all this?

Truth to tell, though, it was the late hours spent trying to figure out his latest puzzle, one that Rohan had helped him discover...

"I will try to get more sleep, Nurse Guilder."

The nurse nodded in satisfaction, made a final notation and hung up the clipboard. "Are you going to be here awhile longer?"

"If that's all right."

"Of course."

Even if Michael left, his thoughts wouldn't stray far from Rohan Wallace. His guilt had kept him from accompanying his wife, Molly, to the harbor where she was picking up Rohan's grandmother.

"I was told that Detective Chief Inspector Paddington has managed to find this poor soul's family," Nurse Guilder said.

"He has." Michael knew she was pumping him for information. Part of him resented that, but he realized that gossip and stories were the lifeblood of a little town like Blackpool.

Besides that, he wanted to counteract the idea the local citizens had of Rohan Wallace as a thief. No one yet knew what he had been doing at Crowe's Nest, the ancestral home of the Crowe family, or why Aleister Crowe had shot him. Michael felt certain it had something to do with the model of the original town of Blackpool that Rohan had helped him construct, based on the one in the library. Their reconstruction had revealed some interesting secrets, but it hadn't revealed them all.

At times when he was feeling morbid, Michael wondered why Crowe hadn't killed Rohan that night. Several months ago, he'd witnessed Aleister Crowe kill a man without hesitation. Except in that instance, he had done it to protect Michael from thugs trying to kill him.

So why had Crowe spared Rohan's life?

The nurse interrupted his thoughts. "Is Mr. Wallace's family coming to see him?"

"His grandmother is on her way now." Michael flicked a glance at the clock on the wall. "She should be here anytime. My wife went down to the harbor to meet her."

"Such a young man." Nurse Guilder shook her head sorrowfully and looked at the figure on the bed. "This is going to be a hard thing for a grandmother to see, even knowing he'll live. I've got two grandchildren of my own. Like angels, they are. I wouldn't want any kind of harm to come to them, no matter what mischief they got themselves into."

"No." Michael studied the beeping, clicking machines that watched over Rohan while he remained in the coma. "He's healing nicely?"

"Of course. Doctor Timms is absolutely brilliant at his craft. If I had to get shot, he's the very man I'd want working on me." Nurse Guilder paused at the door. "There's a fresh pot of tea put on if you want some."

Michael let his empty cup hang from a finger against his jeans and gave her a smile. "Maybe in a bit."

She left.

Anxious, he walked over to the bed and stared down at the man who'd been both friend and confidant to him. One didn't always mean the other. Rohan Wallace was different. Michael had sensed that from the start, and he'd learned to pay attention to the things Rohan knew. Even without understanding exactly how he knew them.

In the past five days, Rohan had lost weight, despite the constant saline and glucose IV bags. He was nearly Michael's age, somewhere in his early thirties, and wore dreadlocks. His ebony skin had a warm cocoa luster, and scars from past physical encounters marked his arms and shoulders. A tube ran up his nose and bandages swathed his chest under the thin hospital gown.

Rohan had been—*was,* Michael insisted—a physical man. His callused hands revealed a long and intimate acquaintanceship with hard work. He was quick to laugh and quick to joke. And he had never hesitated to cover Michael's back.

Michael took his iPhone mobile device from his pocket and texted his wife. Molly probably wouldn't be able to hear the phone at the marina. With the archaeologists still mucking about after the discovery of the slaver the *Seaclipse,* the marina was a noisy place.

GRANDMOTHER?

To his surprise, Molly's reply was almost instant.

PLANE'S COMING NOW. TALK TO YOU SOON.

Opening the digital photo album on his iPhone, Michael studied the three-dimensional model he and Rohan had made of Blackpool. He had been intrigued by and noticed that the older buildings had enjoyed special relationships with each other, and then realized that the sides were designed to fold in on themselves to create a cube. He believed the cube was a three-dimensional map, but of what? Where did it lead? Each of the cube sides also held geometric markings: a square, a triangle, a pentagon and others. But again, he had no idea what they meant.

Blackpool had begun its life as a smuggler's port, a dream harbor where stolen goods could be swapped, stored and sold. In the 1700s, pirates had considered the town a haven, and legitimate businesses had sprung up in short order. Inns and taverns and eating places had manifested first, quickly followed by a blacksmith's forge, a cooper's shop, a carpenter's workshop and a ship-repair business.

Glancing out the window, he stared down at the harbor. Professor Hume-Thorson's graduate students still worked at the site where the *Seaclipse* had gone down.

The slave ship remained out of reach for an in-depth study and hadn't yet given up all her secrets. Enough surprises, though, had spilled out to start tongues wagging throughout Blackpool. Several marina businesses remained angry at the continuing marine investigation. Only two days ago, local sailors had gotten into a proper donnybrook with the archaeology crew. From all accounts, the professor had proven himself quite capable at fisticuffs. The locals now had a grudging respect for the newcomers.

The marina's makeover was progressing, too, though it would be a while before things were finished. Blackpool was in a state of transition, and many of the citizens blamed Molly, his wife, because she'd been responsible for securing the grant money that had enabled the renovations to go forward.

In a way, Michael had to admit that the feeling was justified. Molly had helped engineer a lot of changes in Blackpool, but most were ones that residents wanted or thought necessary. Such as the marina remodel. The problem was that most folks wanted the changes to happen in the blink of an eye. The town hated anything that impeded the pace of everyday life.

Michael turned away from the window and wished he could just as easily turn away from the guilt that plagued him. Rohan lay unmoving on the bed. *Why did you go to Crowe's Nest that night? What were you hoping to prove? What did you see in our model that I haven't yet?*

Those questions gnawed relentlessly at Michael. He was used to being consumed by his imagination. He'd designed award-winning video games for years. He loved problems, and he loved solving them. But the conundrum Rohan had created was—at present—unsolvable. That rankled.

Coming up with a game-logic problem, designing an appropriate level, figuring out a story line that would prompt a player to think in the right direction—all of these things depended on how clever Michael was. Real-world mysteries demanded a whole new realm of patience and perseverance.

He sighed and rolled his neck. Then he noticed the man standing quietly in the doorway.

The aristocratic profile and the widow's peak made Aleister Crowe instantly stand out in a crowd. He was approximately Michael's age, in his early thirties, and was an inch or so shorter. Michael was built broader and more muscular, but Crowe was a predatory wolf. The walking stick he carried with the silver crow as a handle was an affectation rather than an aid, but it also set him apart from others. As always, he wore an immaculate black suit. Today he had a bloodred tea rose in his lapel. It made Michael suspect the man had come from a lunch engagement with a woman.

Somehow the thought that Crowe had been out pursuing a potential love interest before coming to the hospital made his presence there even more egregious.

"Did you come round hoping your little friend might whisper secrets into your ear?" Crowe's cold gaze pierced Michael.

"What are you doing here?" Instinctively, Michael walked around the bed and put himself between Rohan and Crowe.

"The last I'd heard, Paddington still wasn't handcuffing Wallace to the bed. I wanted to make sure it was safe to go home."

"You're lying."

Smiling in amusement, Crowe cocked an eyebrow. "You're far too emotional, Michael. You really should get some rest."

Michael made himself breathe slowly.

Crowe looked past him. "Where is your wife?"

"On an errand. I'm surprised you didn't know."

With a shrug, the man twirled his walking stick. "Contrary to your present belief, I don't much care what you and your wife do in Blackpool. I only want to ensure that my family is protected."

"Rohan didn't go there that night to hurt you."

"Then maybe you'd care to tell me why that man was sneaking through my house? How he managed to steal past a very sophisticated security system?"

Michael didn't have an answer.

Crowe nodded arrogantly. "I thought as much." He adjusted the tea rose in his lapel, then started to walk out of the room. "Take care, Michael. These lost causes you and your wife have a habit of chasing after might one day turn around and bite you."

CHAPTER TWO

THE BRIGHT YELLOW FLOATPLANE bobbed in the air as it fought turbulence. Getting to Blackpool was difficult by road, and the floatplane service was the quickest mode of transportation.

Shading her eyes even though she wore sunglasses, Molly Graham watched the plane's descent. She stood at the end of the pier that thrust out into the Blackpool harbor. Noise from all the diesel- and petrol-powered engines created a disturbing cacophony that battered her with sonic fists. The salt air stung as it filled her nostrils.

She wore a casual business suit—a dove-gray jacket and skirt with a simple white button-down and a gray herringbone fedora with a white band. She also wore sensible dark gray strappy ankle boots with wide four-inch heels that wouldn't get caught in the planks of the pier. Her handbag matched the shoes. The wind shifted and her dark auburn hair danced across her shoulders.

Irwin Jaeger stood at Molly's side. He was the Grahams' houseman, one of the two full-time employees that came with the manor house she and Michael had purchased. Irwin was thin and in his early seventies and he wore his black livery like a suit of armor. His bushy mustache twitched a little. "Appears to be a bit of a draft up there."

Molly surveyed the water. Chop stirred the surface. "I'm beginning to think we should have picked up Mrs. Myrie in London."

"It was her wish to come with all due speed. If we had picked her up, she wouldn't have arrived in Blackpool until late this evening."

"I know."

"And she did inquire about possible air transport here."

"Yes, but a floatplane? At her age?"

Irwin stiffened slightly. "Might I suggest that age and infirmity don't always go together? That there is nothing wrong with keeping longevity in close orbit with a sense of adventure?"

"Sorry."

Irwin smiled at that and adjusted his thick bifocals. His muddy-brown eyes twinkled. "It could well be that, under other circumstances, Mrs. Myrie might consider flying in a floatplane to be one of her grandest adventures."

Under other circumstances. Molly wished that the visit had been just that. She hadn't gotten to know Rohan Wallace quite as well as Michael had, but she'd liked the man. Over the phone, his grandmother had come across as a darling woman with a large personality.

"Well, let's hope she doesn't have too much adventure." As Molly refocused her attention on the plane, it began to circle, losing speed and altitude.

A moment later, the floatplane splashed into the harbor, hopped a few times, tilted crazily for an instant, then recovered. After a quick adjustment, the aircraft turned and sped toward the pier. The propeller cut the air and powered them forward, skipping over the chop.

When the floatplane neared the pier, Irwin picked up a mooring line. Even before the plane stopped moving forward, the cockpit door opened and a teenager with wild green hair shoved his head and shoulders out. Sunlight gleamed on his facial piercings. He wore a black T-shirt that had a skull in a top hat and black powder pistols crossed under its chin.

Molly groaned. "I can't believe Solomon let Rory fly Mrs. Myrie out here. I specifically asked him to do it himself."

On occasion, she and Michael had hired Solomon Crates to fly them into London. Generally that was only on days that Michael had to handle some emergency meeting at his video-game company.

Rory caught the line when Irwin threw it, then used both hands to haul the plane toward the pier. "Hallo, Mrs. G." He waved enthusiastically.

"Hello, Rory. Where's your dad?"

"Himself is back at home. Mother insisted on eating something different last night." Rory grinned, looking every bit of twelve though Molly knew he was at least sixteen. "From all indications, the sushi didn't agree with him. He couldn't bring Mrs. Myrie over, so he asked me to." He made a "tah-dah" gesture. "So here we are. And I gotta admit, she's quite the flyer."

"After that rough landing, I'll be surprised if she ever considers flying again." Molly tried to peer into the plane.

Rory put a finger to his lips and held up a hand. He smiled encouragingly. "I thought it was a good landing myself." He waved for Molly to agree.

"Don't make no excuses for me, young man," came a voice from the plane. "That was one of the worst landings I've made in a while. But it's been years since I had the chance to land a plane, so I thank you for the opportunity."

Incredulous, Molly stared as Rory dropped down to the floating dock and reached back toward the door.

Nanny Myrie, Rohan's grandmother, appeared in the doorway. She wasn't exactly what Molly had imagined when she'd talked to the woman over the phone. She was around five feet tall and full figured. White hair with dark charcoal streaks framed a round, golden-brown face. She wore a colorful blue-and-green dress and a silver necklace.

"That landing wasn't none of this boy's fault." Nanny reached down to take Rory's hand.

"What are you talking about?" Rory gently helped the woman onto the dock. "That was a fantastic bit of flyin', Mrs. M. Absolutely brill. I was never worried for a minute."

"*You* flew the plane?" Molly gaped at the older woman.

Beside her, Irwin stifled a laugh, failed and had to cover it with a cough. "Pardon me. I had something in my throat."

"I did fly the plane." Nanny Myrie crossed the floating dock with ease and climbed the ladder to the pier without pause. "I haven't had the opportunity in a long time. It brought back a lot of memories. Good memories."

Irwin offered his hand and the woman took it. He helped her up to the pier and introduced himself.

"You're Mrs. Graham?" The woman turned to Molly.

"I am. But please call me Molly." With a smile, she shook her hand.

The older woman's grip was firm and strong and rough with calluses. "Molly, you may call me Nanny."

"Of course."

"You're American, correct?"

"Yes."

"But your husband's not? He didn't sound American when I talked with him on the phone."

"Right, Michael is British."

"You'll have to tell me how you two met sometime." Nanny rubbed the back of Molly's hand. "I'm sure there's a story there."

"There is."

"I appreciate you and your husband flying me in."

"It's our pleasure."

"Well, I just wanted you to know that. Once I learned Rohan was here in the hospital, I had to find a way to get to him. I'm all the family that boy has left."

At the sadness in Nanny's voice, Molly's heart went out to the woman. "I'm sure Rohan feels very lucky."

Nanny's hand tightened on Molly's briefly. She looked past her to the harbor. "Awfully busy place."

"There's a lot going on right now."

"The policeman I talked to—"

"Detective Chief Inspector Maurice Paddington."

Nanny nodded. "Yes, that's the one. He said that you're responsible for a lot of this."

Thank you for that, Inspector Paddington. "Unfortunately I seem to have stirred up more than I'd thought possible." Molly was a grant writer. Usually she worked for nonprofit companies, as she had with the projects in Blackpool, but she'd also worked with corporate entities for a percentage. Her success had enabled her to take an early retirement, and one that she felt was well deserved after all her hard work.

Keeping up the pace she'd had before she'd met Michael wouldn't have allowed the close marriage they had now. Michael had stepped away from much of his design work for the same reasons. Both of them had enough money invested to be financially stable for the rest of their lives. But they also picked up the occasional project that appealed to them. Michael hadn't quit working on his own brands, though he did turn the games out at a slower rate these days.

"Mr. Paddington seems to think that some of the things you and your husband have been interested in might be what got my grandson in trouble."

Molly searched the woman's dark eyes but found no accusation there. "To be honest, Michael and I don't know what Rohan was doing at the Crowe house that night."

"The policeman led me to believe Rohan was friends with your husband."

"They were. They *are*. Michael likes Rohan a lot. They've been working on a project together."

"What project?"

"I'm sure Michael will show you if you want to see it. Explaining it just isn't the same."

Nanny nodded.

"But Rohan didn't tell us much, I'm afraid," Molly added. "He was a very private person."

"That boy has always been too quiet. Always thinking, always with his head up in the clouds. Never could get nothing out of him unless he was ready to talk about it."

Molly wanted to turn the conversation to a lighter

subject. "Speaking of up in the clouds, where did you learn to fly a floatplane?"

Nanny smiled. "In Kingston. I did crop dusting for farmers and I hauled tourists around in helicopters."

"You fly helicopters, too?"

"Not anymore. But I probably still can. It's not something you forget how to do."

Rory passed the woman's bags up to Irwin, then clambered up to help Irwin carry them to the waiting vintage limousine. The luxury car had come with the house, as well, and Michael and Molly seldom used it. However, Irwin loved taking it out every chance he got. He'd absolutely insisted on driving it to pick up their guest.

"Have you seen my grandson today, Molly?"

"Only a short time ago. We left Michael at the hospital with him." Molly hesitated. "Michael's been to visit Rohan at least once every day."

"He's a good friend to my grandbaby."

"Michael's a good person."

"This thing that happened to Rohan, it must be hard on your husband."

"It is."

Nanny looked out across the harbor, but Molly knew the woman wasn't seeing the ships and the buildings around the marina. She felt certain Nanny Myrie was thinking about that little boy Rohan Wallace had once been.

"The most difficult question for Michael is why Rohan was at the Crowes' house that night." Molly spoke softly, hoping not to offend. "Michael keeps wanting to blame himself. I've tried to talk to him about it, but until he finds out what happened, I'm afraid he's going to remain disconsolate."

Turning back to Molly, Nanny patted her on the arm. "Don't you be fretting too much about that husband of yours, Molly. I can tell you now, just like I'll tell your Michael—this had nothing to do with some project. Rohan was obsessed with digging into the Crowes. That's why he came all this way. The paths of that family and mine crossed a long time ago."

"What do you mean?"

"Rohan didn't end up in Blackpool by chance, Molly. He came here for a reason. Let's get to the hospital and I'll tell you and your husband about it. Ain't no reason for him to be feeling responsible one minute longer."

The woman's declaration lifted some of the dread from Molly's heart. She hated not knowing what was going on, and she hated the fact that Michael felt it was his fault.

"Ladies, the car is ready." Irwin stood politely waiting.

Nanny stuck her arm through Molly's and they walked up the pier toward the waiting car. Sensing someone watching her, Molly glanced up at the marina. Most, if not all, of the town knew who she was, but there were a number of tourists in Blackpool, as well.

A long-haired young man in dark clothes stood staring at her. Even when she caught him looking at her, he didn't turn away. He just grinned, but there was no mirth in his expression. Judging by the black leather jacket, tattoos and facial piercings, he was one of Stefan Draghici's gypsy family. The Draghici family had shown up in Blackpool several months ago claiming that the Crowe family owed them a fortune in Romanian gold that had been stolen from their ancestors.

"Irwin." Molly reached into her jacket pocket for her iPhone.

"I see him, miss."

"Do you recognize him?"

"No."

"Was he there before?"

"This is the first I've noticed him." Irwin paused. "I don't think we're in for any trouble. There are too many people in the vicinity."

And if he was going to do something, he would have done it already. Molly knew that was what Irwin hadn't said. The thought chilled her even more than the breeze blowing in off the sea. She blinked and the young man was gone.

CHAPTER THREE

IN THE HOSPITAL LOUNGE, Michael helped himself to a cup of tea while he talked to Keith over his iPhone. Keith was a good friend and the primary artist on the current video game they were designing. The game revolved around an underwater fantasy world filled with fantastic creatures, mermaids and adventure. Lots and lots of adventure. At present, they were working on a downloadable-content episode to add to the original game. "No, no, loved the sketches of the undersea city, mate."

"So what's your problem, then?" Keith sounded irritable, but that was because he'd just gotten up. "Something must be wrong."

"Nobody said anything was wrong with them. Didn't you get my notes?"

Keith sighed. "I got your *book,* if that's what you emailed me. A note, Michael, is something that fits on a Post-it. Or a three-by-five-inch index card. That's a bloody note. What you sent me was a freaking history."

"Sorry. I thought maybe you'd want to see the document. It has a detailed history of the city."

"I'm not a reader, Michael. I'm a graphic guy. If a story can't be told in pictures, I'm not interested."

"And if it's over ten minutes long. Yeah, yeah, I

remember. Short attention span. You know, your romantic life must be a mess." Michael added a scone to his tea saucer.

"My romantic life is just fine. I'm sure Katrina can provide a glowing recommendation if you're interested." Katrina was Keith's significant other. She was organized and neat, the exact opposite of Keith. "In twenty-five words or less, what do you want me to do with the concepts of the city?"

"Older."

"Older?"

"The buildings need to be older. The edges are too defined. There aren't enough barnacles and age spots. And there should be scars from past wars. Gaps and missing pieces."

"Ah. See? You could have just said that in your email."

Chagrined, Michael knew it was true. He hadn't been focused. He'd been distracted. He still was. Only, now he was thinking about the encounter with Aleister Crowe and alternative ways he could have responded.

"So where's your head at, Michael?"

"Just sorting through things."

"Your friend's shooting still bothering you?"

"I haven't forgotten about it."

"Maybe I should wander up that way for a few days."

Michael smiled at the thought. "You? In Blackpool? Aside from the fact that Molly would be afraid you'd get us strung up on the nearest yardarm, you wouldn't last a day before you'd go as mad as a hatter."

"You have such little faith."

"I know you and I love you, mate. You're a brother to me. I appreciate the offer, but there's nothing you can do here."

"If that changes, you'll tell me?"

"The very instant."

"Okay. Well, in the meantime, I'll age your city."

"By thousands of years. It should be literally on the verge of turning to dust on the seafloor."

"Got it. I'll work it up and get it back to you."

"Soon?"

Keith laughed. "Soon enough."

"I want the city to be the only thing aging."

Keith groaned good-naturedly. "Thought you were retired and away from all the deadline pressure. Just for fun, you said. Just to keep your hand in."

"I meant that, but we've still got people waiting on us for work so they can keep cashing paychecks." That was the secondary reason for keeping the studio alive. The primary one was because Michael couldn't stop imagining games. There were just too many interesting things in the world. Actually, worlds. And a lot of them were always traipsing through his mind.

"Give me a week, mate, and I'll present you with a much older undersea city."

"I'm looking forward to it." Michael rang off and started to pocket his mobile, but it buzzed to signal a new text.

I HAVE NANNY MYRIE. DID YOU KNOW SHE CAN FLY A FLOATPLANE?

Michael shook his head. He couldn't imagine Rohan Wallace's grandmother at all, much less as a floatplane pilot. He slid his iPhone into his jeans and headed back to his friend's room.

A MAN STOOD BY ROHAN'S BED when Michael reached the open door. About six feet tall and thirtyish, he had chestnut-brown hair pulled into a small ponytail. A dragon tattoo snaked up from the collar of the dark blue suit jacket he wore. His jeans were tucked into motorcycle boots.

"Rohan. C'mon, mate, I need you to wake up." The man's voice held a desperate note. "You're leaving me hanging here. These guys I've got chasing after me aren't messing about."

Moving quietly, Michael put the teacup and saucer onto the small window shelf by the door. "Who are you?"

The man whirled around. Wild-eyed and breathing fast, he stared at Michael. "Just checking on my mate. That's all. Nothing to get your knickers in a twist over."

Michael spread his hands away from his sides to show that he meant no harm. "My name's Michael Graham."

The man's eyes widened slightly. "I know who you are. I'll ask you to clear that door."

Slowly, Michael shook his head. "Not until you give me some identification."

The man grinned, but it was a sick expression and tainted with panic. "You don't need that."

"Sorry. I don't succumb to Jedi mind tricks. But I will be having your name."

"Let me introduce you to Mr. Slicey." With a quick snap of his wrist, the man pulled a switchblade knife into view. He flipped it open as easily as breathing and the stainless-steel edge gleamed. It would have been an excellent cut-scene in a game. "I don't want to hurt you, but I will if I have to. I don't have time for a lot of questions."

His stomach twisting and turning sour with fear, Michael raised his hands. Until moving to Blackpool, he'd led a rather dull life when it came to criminal affairs. But recently he'd been threatened, beaten and shot at. He wasn't becoming any more inured to violence—his quivering stomach was the perfect illustration of that fact— but he was determined that he wasn't going to allow any information this man might have about what Rohan was doing in Crowe's Nest that night to slip through his fingers.

"Stand aside." The man held the switchblade before him.

"Can't do that, I'm afraid. I need to know what business you've had with my friend."

"None of yours."

"I'll have to be the judge of that."

Smoothly and without hesitation, the man lunged forward, his body following the knife. Reacting instinctively, reflexes honed from rugby and other sports he'd played, Michael slapped the man's hand away. The fellow tried to slip through the door, but Michael slammed his body into his attacker's and bounced him off the door frame.

Off balance and slightly dazed, the thug swept the knife back at Michael, who managed to grab the man's wrist in both hands, but not before the blade sliced through his rugby jersey and burned across his stomach. Twisting viciously, Michael experienced a momentary thrill of success as the switchblade clattered to the floor. He took just a second to kick the weapon under Rohan's bed, then the man head-butted him in the face.

The room and the lights swam in Michael's vision and pain filled his skull. He managed to stay upright despite the dizziness that surged through him. He felt blood running down his face and stomach and told himself he was a proper cretin for trying to mix it up with a man with a knife.

Then his attacker slammed a shoulder into him and knocked him backward. Before Michael could recover, the man shoved him out of the way and ran. Staggering, senses reeling, Michael followed.

MERCIFUL ANGELS WAS SMALL. The second-floor nurses' station was in the center of the building next to the flight of stairs leading down. Hospital rooms lined halls on either side of the large area. Frightened nurses stepped back from the man as he ran. Michael trailed at his heels and, with his longer strides, gained steadily.

Grabbing the low wall near the stairs, the man whipped around it and took the stairway down to the first floor. Two nurses shouted out in alarm and Michael felt certain security would be alerted. That suited him fine, although the guards he'd seen were all elderly gentlemen and didn't look as if they'd put up much of a fight. He hoped that Paddington or one of Blackpool's constables would be nearby. With all the work going on in the marina and the shipwreck discovery, extra men were on duty.

Losing his attacker at the first landing, Michael panicked for a moment till he made the corner and spotted the guy streaking for the front door. By the time the man reached it, Michael was closing the distance again.

The man burst through the door and ran outside into the small yard. Merciful Angels was only a couple blocks back of Main Street and fronted a residential area filled with small, old houses. The tiny visitors' parking lot in front of the hospital was barely large enough to hold six vehicles. Both of the town's ambulances sat at the emergency-room entrance.

The streets in Blackpool were small and narrow, built more for wagons and carts than sedans. The citizens got around on bicycles, mopeds and motorbikes. Very few had cars, and only a handful of businesses used delivery vans.

Up to full speed now, the fleeing man sped toward the parked cars. One of them was Aleister Crowe's green Jaguar. Crowe stood to the side of the vehicle, talking on his mobile.

Another man stood near Crowe. He was about Crowe's age and prim, dressed in a gunmetal-gray business suit with neatly coiffed blond hair and amber-tinted aviator sunglasses.

Drawing closer to his quarry, Michael launched himself forward and grabbed for the man's feet. He succeeded in wrapping an arm around his knees and the two of them went down in a sprawl. Just before they hit the ground, Michael heard a sudden, harsh crack.

He knew immediately something was wrong. The man fell too loosely. Normally a person would tighten up a little even if he'd been trained professionally to fall.

Rolling to his feet, Michael kept one hand locked around the man's ankle so he wouldn't get away. One glance at the man assured him that wouldn't be the case. A trickle of blood slid down his attacker's cheek and dripped off his nose from a round wound on his temple.

Stunned, Michael couldn't help but stare for a moment, then he ran for cover beside the cars.

"What the bloody hell is going on?" The man who had been standing with Crowe was now huddled beside him, holding his arms protectively over his head.

"Sniper." Michael fumbled for his iPhone and got it out.

Crowe shifted, turning on his feet while remaining in a crouched position. "One sniper or more?"

Michael shook his head. "Don't know." He punched the speed dial for the Blackpool police station. Since he and Molly had started helping the police solve murders, he'd kept the number ready.

"Were they after you or the other man?" Crowe asked.

"Whoever shot him got his target."

"Are you wounded?"

"I don't think so." The mobile began to ring while Michael patted himself down.

"You're bleeding."

"Had a disagreement with that bloke before we turned it into a footrace."

"Who was the dead man?"

"I have no idea." Michael scanned the surrounding houses, wondering if the sniper was already moving into a more advantageous position.

Mercifully, his call was answered. "Blackpool police station. State the nature of your emergency."

"This is Michael Graham. A man has just been shot dead at Merciful Angels. Ring DCI Paddington, would you?" He spoke much more calmly and rationally than he felt. What had the man been doing in Rohan Wallace's room? How had Rohan left the man hanging? And who was after him? Had the sniper only been shooting at the dead man? Or was Michael a target, too?

CHAPTER FOUR

"HAVE YOU AND YOUR HUSBAND lived here long?"

Seated in the limousine's plush backseat, Molly gazed at Blackpool with affection. "No, not long. We both came from big cities—Michael from London, and I grew up in Queens. We actually met in Los Angeles, if you can believe that, and we were torn about where to live. But when we saw Blackpool, we knew we had to live here. At least for a while."

Nanny Myrie nodded. "So this is not where you'll be putting down roots."

Molly frowned a little at that and felt uncomfortable. "I don't think 'putting down roots' is something either of us has thought about. Our adult lives have been so hectic, always running after one deadline or another, that we just wanted to slow things down for a while."

"Have you?" Nanny peered at her expectantly.

"Slowed things down?"

"Yes."

Thinking back over the past few months and the constant barrage of riddles, mysteries and murders that had complicated their lives, Molly shook her head. "Not really. But it hasn't been for lack of trying."

A knowing smile spread across Nanny's face. "I'm afraid you may find that life doesn't really slow down.

Especially if you have a tendency toward adventure anyway."

A siren swooped in from behind them.

Glancing back over her shoulder as Irwin discreetly pulled to the side, Molly watched in astonishment as one of the Blackpool police units roared past the limousine.

Nanny stiffened and stared anxiously after the departing police cruiser. "That vehicle seems to be heading in the same direction we are."

"Yes, it does." Molly opened her handbag and took out her iPhone. She punched Michael's name and waited as panic stretched within her. All the horrible things she'd experienced over the past months came clamoring back. She willed Michael to answer his cell.

He picked up almost immediately, sounding tense. "Molly? Are you all right?"

"Yes. Why, has something happened?"

Michael's sigh of relief was audible. "There's been a bit of a skirmish at the hospital. Perhaps it would be better if you took Mrs. Myrie somewhere and waited till things calm down here."

"I don't think so." Molly wasn't going to do that until she saw for herself that Michael was healthy and in one piece.

"Then again, maybe you're right. You might be safer here. Until we can figure out who the dead man is and why he was killed."

"Mr. Graham." Molly recognized the voice of DCI Paddington. He sounded irritated and officious. "It would be better if we didn't go about announcing everything for the world to hear. The investigation might be less of a bother. We certainly have no end of lollygaggers and looky-loos standing about as it is."

"Molly, I'm sure you've got a hundred questions, but the inspector's beside himself. I love you."

"I love you, too. We'll be there in just a moment."

Michael sighed. "I'll be glad to see you, but I can't speak for the inspector. Ta."

Before Molly could say goodbye, Michael had broken the connection. She slid the phone back into her handbag.

"Something is wrong?" Nanny gazed at Molly with soulful eyes.

"Rohan's situation hasn't changed, but a man has been murdered. The inspector won't let Michael say more than that." Straining anxiously to look ahead, she saw the rooftop of Merciful Angels. In the next moment, she spotted the police cars surrounding the small parking area. Instant relief washed through her when she recognized Michael standing there.

IRWIN PARKED THE CAR AS CLOSE to the activity as he could, but Sergeant Luann Krebs and one of the temporary constables were putting up crime-scene tape to secure the area.

Officious and no-nonsense as ever, Krebs held up a hand as Molly got out of the limousine. A frown darkened the woman's square-jawed face. Her short blond hair moved slightly in the breeze. "I'll have to ask you to stay there, Mrs. Graham."

"I want to see my husband." Molly worked hard to keep the panic from her voice.

Krebs put one hand on her uniform belt and jerked

her other thumb over her shoulder. "We can't disturb the site of the shooting. I can assure you that he's fine."

"He told me that much over the phone."

Krebs shook her head. "Mr. Graham is being questioned. He shouldn't be giving out information over his mobile." She reached for the walkie-talkie at her belt.

Exasperated, Molly leaned a hip against the limousine.

The locals had turned out by the dozens. They stood just beyond the yellow tape and collapsible sawhorses used to mark the scene. All of them talked and gestured, pointing to the parking area.

A man's body lay sprawled across the small lot but Molly had lost sight of Michael. Then she spotted Paddington. The Detective Chief Inspector was a large man but carried his weight well because he was broad shouldered. He paced in front of a Jaguar that looked suspiciously like Aleister Crowe's and pulled at his fierce mustache. The inspector was in quite the mood, just as Michael had said.

"Does anyone know the identity of the man that was shot?" Molly asked Krebs, amazed she was calm enough to pose such a question.

Krebs pursed her lips before answering. "That's police business, Mrs. Graham. I'm afraid I'm not at liberty to say." Her eyes locked on Nanny Myrie. "Is this Mr. Wallace's family?"

"His grandmother, yes. Mrs. Nanny Myrie."

A moment passed as Krebs considered the situation. "I think it would be a good idea if you and Mrs. Myrie went into the hospital. I know the inspector will want to talk to you, Mrs. Myrie." The sergeant lifted the crime-scene tape. "Come along now."

Talk to us or grill us? Molly wondered. Based on past experience with the inspector, she knew Paddington tended toward surly when upset. Reluctantly, Molly guided Nanny under the tape and toward the hospital.

PERCHED ON THE EDGE of Paddington's car fender, Michael was glad most of his panic had subsided. Residual adrenaline still made his hands shake, but for the most part he was again in control of himself. He'd examined the knife wound and judged it to be minor, the bleeding already stopped.

"You're sure you've never seen the dead man before today?" Paddington stood in front of Michael. The effort it took for the man to remain still made him almost vibrate. He kept his hands busy with his pipe.

"I'm sure."

"But he knew Rohan Wallace."

"He knew Rohan's name. He called him 'mate.' But I couldn't testify to how close their relationship was."

Paddington puffed thoughtfully on his pipe. "He said Rohan left him hanging?"

"That's what I heard."

"And that people were looking for him?"

"Yes." Michael was conscious of the microrecorder in the inspector's pocket. He felt sick, and his awareness of the body lying only a short distance away felt more and more disturbing.

"He didn't happen to say why they were looking for him?"

Michael gestured at his bruised face. "There wasn't much time for chatting, Inspector. I walked in on him and he made to leave. I tried to stop him."

"Why would you do that, Mr. Graham? You could just as easily have allowed him to go."

Surprised, Michael considered that. Then he thought about why the inspector might have asked the question and pointed out the option. "I want to know what happened to Rohan. That man, whoever he was, offered an opportunity to find out."

"What made you so sure of that?"

"I wasn't. We didn't get very far into the discussion when he pulled a knife on me. A switchblade. You'll find it under Rohan's bed."

Paddington glanced at one of the policemen beside him. "Be a good lad and go secure that weapon."

The policeman nodded and left.

Paddington swiveled his gaze back to Michael. "Rohan Wallace was shot while burgling the Crowe home."

"I'm not satisfied that's the whole truth of the matter."

A short distance away, Aleister Crowe slid off his vehicle and approached Michael, thrusting an angry finger in his direction. "What are you trying to say? That I deliberately shot a man with no justification?"

Blood boiling with renewed anger, Michael stood and faced Crowe. "Did you?"

"No."

"No one found a weapon on Rohan that night, Crowe."

"You can strangle a man with your bare hands while he's sleeping."

"It's not as fast as shooting people, though, is it?"

Crowe took another step forward and Michael automatically raised his hands in defense.

Quick as a fox, Crowe's blond companion stepped

between Michael and Crowe and held Crowe back. "Aleister. *Aleister.* Listen to me. You're not doing yourself any good here. Let it go."

Paddington had placed a big hand in the middle of Michael's chest, but focused on the blond man. "Who are you?"

"Lockwood Nightingale."

"What business did you have here today, Mr. Nightingale?"

"I'm a friend of Mr. Crowe's."

"Really?"

Breathing hard, Michael retreated to Paddington's car.

Paddington shifted his attention to Crowe. "You often meet your friends at the hospital, Mr. Crowe?"

"I was here on business, Inspector." Nightingale straightened his jacket and smiled.

"What business might that be?"

Crowe leaned in, his face tight with anger. "My business, and none of yours."

Nightingale spoke in a soft voice. "Easy, Aleister. Let me handle this. Please."

With an oath, Crowe turned away.

"I was here today as a favor to Aleister, Inspector Paddington." Nightingale reached into his inside jacket pocket and took out an engraved cardholder. He flipped the holder open with a practiced flourish and produced an expensive embossed card. "I'm a solicitor."

Paddington took the card and examined it. "Do you feel you need a solicitor, Mr. Crowe?"

Crowe started to make a scathing reply, judging from the apoplectic expression he wore, then subsided when Nightingale raised a hand.

"I advised Mr. Crowe that he might want to seek counsel regarding the shooting incident in his home." Nightingale put the cardholder away.

"No charges have been brought against Mr. Crowe."

Nightingale smiled unctuously. "We have two matters before us, Inspector. I believe the criminal matter has been put to rest, and that Mr. Crowe acted in the best interests of his family when he shot a trespasser in his home."

Michael started to object, but Paddington raised an admonishing hand without looking in his direction. Bitterly, Michael swallowed his comments.

"But I also advised Mr. Crowe that Rohan Wallace's family might seek to place fiduciary responsibility on him in civil court. We met here today so that I could deliver a court order to have copies of the injured man's hospital reports released to me. In case we end up in court over the matter. A little prejudicial caution, I admit."

"Rohan hasn't had any family to speak up for him," Michael said before Paddington could wave him to silence.

"But that isn't the case anymore, is it? Mr. Wallace's grandmother has arrived in Blackpool."

Paddington raised an eyebrow. "How do you know that, Mr. Nightingale?"

The solicitor shrugged. "I witnessed her arrival only a few moments ago. I heard your sergeant acknowledge her." He pointed toward the limousine.

Irwin stood at the front of the vehicle like a soldier at his post. Michael almost smiled at that; the man's dedication to his vocation was reassuring.

"Therefore, Inspector, lines on this battlefront are changing."

Michael gazed down at the dead man and couldn't agree more.

Paddington's mobile rang and he pulled it from his hip holster. He said his name and listened briefly, then closed the mobile and put it away. He glanced at Michael. "It appears they found the spot where the shots came from. Would you like to come along?"

"You're asking me?"

"You needn't if you don't wish to."

"No. I'd be happy to come. This just isn't the kind of thing you'd normally invite me to."

"This, Mr. Graham, doesn't appear to be a normal day."

CHAPTER FIVE

"THE SHOOTER STOOD HERE, Inspector, and he had a clear view of the hospital."

Michael didn't recognize the serious middle-aged man in the Blackpool Police uniform. He assumed he was one of the temporary officers that were helping out during the remodel of the marina. With all the new people in town, as well as the supplies and equipment, extra security had been necessary.

The officer looked earnest and neat as a pin. His short-cropped hair was barely longer than the stubble Michael wore. Creases showed in the corners of his eyes and lightly on his forehead. His tan was deep, burned into his flesh by years of working in the sun.

"Tell me your name."

"Watts, Inspector. Trevor Watts."

"Ah, yes." Paddington nodded in satisfaction. "You're the lad with exotic military training."

"Yes, sir. I did a bit with the Special Air Service. Mustered out honorably with injuries a few years back."

Michael was impressed. The SAS was England's foremost special-forces unit. The team had seen action around the globe and were noted for their thoroughness and precision.

"SAS, eh?" Paddington gazed out the bedroom window of the second-floor flat they were in across from the hospital. Other than a few trees, the view was clear. "Then I'd assume you know something of shooting like this."

"Yes, sir. I was extremely proficient."

Paddington pointed his pipe at the spot where the dead man had gone down. "How far away would you say the target was?"

"Seven hundred seventy-eight yards, sir."

"That's awfully exact, Officer."

Watts reached into a small bag on his belt and took out micro-size binoculars. "Opti-Logic Sabre II laser rangefinder. Good out to a thousand yards. After I saw that shot, I thought I might need this, so I got it out of my car."

Michael's curiosity was piqued. "What about the shot told you that you might need that device?"

"The round hit the man, correct, Mr. Graham?"

Michael nodded.

"Seven hundred and seventy-eight yards, though I didn't know the exact measurement at the time, plus the fact that the bullet ripped through the victim's apricot tipped me to the fact that we were probably dealing with an experienced sniper. That's why I started scouting the buildings that fit the trajectory and the field of fire."

"'Apricot'?"

"Yes, sir. The medulla oblongata. Located at the base of the skull. Controls involuntary movement. Ensures an instant kill. You put a bullet through that, or the second cervical vertebra, and whomever you shoot is checked out of the festivities."

"You make the shooter sound like he was really good."

"He was, sir. No doubt about it. To pop a man like

that, while he's on the run? Bloody good, sir, and that's the bottom line."

Michael watched the man and wondered what he did when he wasn't hanging about Blackpool, helping with security. He suspected it was generally something a lot more demanding, and they were lucky to have him.

Only then did Michael realize that Paddington had been carefully watching him throughout the exchange. Michael let out a breath and shook his head. "You knew the shooter could have killed me, too."

"The thought crossed my mind simply because the shot that killed that poor devil was so accurately placed and you emerged without a scratch." Paddington glanced around the bedroom. "I felt you should know what you were truly facing today."

Michael's knees were suddenly weak. "Do you mind if I take a seat?"

Watts pointed to a chair at a small computer desk. "There. Please stay out of the way. And if you're going to be sick, please do so in the bin there." He pointed to the small metal rectangle under the desk.

In order to forestall the sick pulsing in his stomach, Michael focused on the room. Judging from the pictures tucked into the bulletin board on the wall, the flat's renter was a young woman interested in music. Stills of Lady Gaga were displayed prominently. "Where's the room's occupant?"

"At Coffey's Garage where she works."

"She was there during the shooting?"

"Her employer confirmed that the young woman has been at work since eight this morning. Constantly in his sight."

Trying to forget about the sniping incident, Michael

examined the pictures of a young woman on the bulletin board. He assumed that the flat was hers. "Does she have a boyfriend?"

"One whose hobby includes sniper rifles?" Paddington smiled. "It's not going to be that easy. There is a young man, but he's in London at the moment, applying for a job."

"I suppose you've confirmed that?"

"Talked to him myself, and to his potential employer." Paddington surveyed the hardwood floor.

Watts was down on his hands and knees, shining a torch under the bed. "I've checked, Inspector, but I can't find the man's brass anywhere."

"Policed up after himself?"

Watts resumed standing and seemed put off by the development. "Yes, sir. The man was very thorough. And he got out of here without being seen, according to the residents I've chatted up."

Those residents stood out in the hall, talking to themselves. Michael heard the constant buzz of conversation splashing around the room. If they knew anything, they would tell.

He studied the lock on the door. It was intact and apparently unmarked. So how had the sniper gotten into the room?

"WE'VE GOT A NAME for the dead man." Paddington closed his mobile and slipped it into his jacket pocket as he trotted down the stairs inside the small building. Crime-scene investigators were still going over the flat.

Michael trailed after the inspector, knowing Paddington wouldn't tell him anything till he was ready to.

Over the past few months, the inspector had come to see the Grahams as annoyances. At least, that was the way Michael felt. Paddington tended to be closed off about his work, and Michael respected that. Unfortunately, he and Molly hadn't had much choice about becoming involved.

More gawkers stood outside on the lawn of the building, while another crowd was kept at bay from the corpse in the parking lot by yellow crime-scene tape. The coroner was there, as well, now.

"Grady Dunkirk." At the bottom of the stairs, Paddington looked back up at Michael.

"I've never heard of him."

"Evidently he was quite a friend of Rohan Wallace."

"If he was, I didn't know about it. Wait, why did you say '*a* name'?" The inflection and choice of words made Michael curious.

Paddington was silent for a moment, and Michael didn't think he was going to get an answer.

"I say 'a name' because the one he gave was false. Krebs initiated a background check on the man and the trace ended pretty quickly. He worked on one of the renovation jobs down at the marina, but his paperwork was thin. It would never have held up under a real examination." A rueful look pinched Paddington's broad face. "Unfortunately, with all the remodeling Mrs. Graham has got started at the marina, jobs have been plentiful and there hasn't been time to see who's who."

Michael bridled at that. Molly's vision for Blackpool was brilliant, and other people in town thought so, too, or none of her ideas would have gotten off the ground.

"Inspector, with all due respect, I don't think Molly is in any way—"

Paddington waved him off. "Don't get your knickers in a twist. That was just an observation."

"Sounded like more than that."

The inspector sighed and wiped his lower face with a handkerchief. "This used to be a comfortable little town, Mr. Graham, before you and your wife moved here. You can take that as you will."

Choosing to ignore the jibe for the moment, Michael asked, "Have you been able to trace the dead man's real identity?"

"We're working on it." The inspector glanced at Michael and lifted an eyebrow. "You're a very good amateur detective, Mr. Graham, and I don't mean to encourage you in any way."

"Believe me, Inspector, if it were up to me, Molly and I would have stayed out of every investigation we've been involved with. What we've experienced—what we've *all* experienced—is just a bit of bad luck at being part of these situations at all."

"Do you think so?"

"Yes."

"Then what was that business with Mr. Crowe earlier?"

Michael shoved his hands in his pockets and met the inspector's gaze full on. "I don't like the man."

"Mr. Crowe does seem to fancy Mrs. Graham's company more than yours."

"Trying to stir up trouble?"

"Jealousy can be a bothersome thing, that's all."

"I'm not jealous of Aleister Crowe's attentiveness to Molly. If there's one thing that's a constant in our world, it's my relationship with my wife." Michael smiled. "The sun will set in the east, Inspector, before I ever doubt Molly."

"You're a lucky man, Mr. Graham." Paddington echoed Michael's smile a little. "I've seen that for myself, and I'm quite certain Mrs. Graham would say the same. But you are not so trusting of Crowe."

Michael shrugged. "I didn't like him before he shot Rohan."

"Rohan Wallace was guilty of breaking and entering into the man's house."

"Rohan wasn't armed."

"As you've seen yourself over these past few months, it doesn't take an armed man to kill a person. Just a very determined one. But you're missing the point, Mr. Graham. A few points, actually."

"Care to enlighten me?"

Paddington smiled. "Thought you'd never ask." He cleared his throat. "Nothing in Mr. Wallace's background suggests that he had the necessary skills to circumvent the state-of-the-art security around Crowe's Nest."

Michael was actually glad to hear the inspector say that.

"I hadn't missed that little fact, Mr. Graham. You and your missus's meddling aside, the Blackpool police department got along quite well before you decided to try your hand at investigatory work."

"I never said you didn't, Inspector."

"So do you know what I've been looking for since Mr. Wallace was shot?"

Michael realized the answer almost immediately. "Someone who could help Rohan break into Crowe's Nest."

"Exactly." Paddington nodded at the group gathered around the body. "Now I have a man, a desperate man by your account, that wished to speak to Mr. Wallace. He's not in the hospital more than a few minutes and he manages to get himself shot. By an expert marksman."

Immediately the pieces fell together in Michael's mind and he chided himself for not seeing it earlier. "An expert marksman. And Rohan needed an expert cracksman to get into Crowe's Nest. You think that once you find out who the dead man truly is, it'll lead you to who the marksman is."

Paddington touched his nose and smiled. "At least, Mr. Graham, I'll have an idea of where to look. Experts tend to know each other."

"If they were friends, why did the shooter kill Grady Dunkirk, or whatever his name turns out to be?"

"You should be able to figure that one out."

"To keep Dunkirk from spilling what he knew?"

Paddington nodded.

"But what?"

"Who he was working for." Paddington shrugged. "Maybe something went missing that night and we haven't heard about it. Maybe someone decided the pie shouldn't be split so many ways. From the sounds of things, you were going to catch Dunkirk. Somebody didn't want him caught."

"Then why allow him to talk to Rohan?"

"Maybe his pallies didn't. Or maybe they made him talk to Rohan. Either way, Dunkirk is dead because of his friends."

"Awfully cold-blooded, don't you think?"

"I do. But that's the kind of work they were in. I have to ask myself, though, how did Rohan Wallace know men such as this?" Paddington looked at Michael. "That was the grandmother with Mrs. Graham, wasn't it?"

"Yes."

"I think I'd like to have a word with her."

CHAPTER SIX

MOLLY SAT IN THE CORNER of Rohan Wallace's hospital room and watched Nanny Myrie softly stroke her grandson's forehead. Rohan didn't respond; the machines kept beeping. Molly hated the helpless feeling that filled her. She also felt intrusive, so she turned her attention to the window.

That wasn't much better. The police cars and the crime-scene tape instantly claimed her attention. She sighed and looked down at the cell phone in her hands. *Michael, where are you?*

"Do you know my grandson well, Molly?"

"Not terribly. He was more Michael's friend than mine. They did all sorts of things together."

"Like what?"

"Sports, mostly. Hiking. Bicycling. Some fishing. Sailing. Those aren't my types of activities. I join Michael occasionally, but he's a much more devoted participant than I am. Rohan gave—gives—him someone to hang with."

"I'm certain he does. Sounds like your man hasn't quite lost touch with the boy he was."

"No, and I don't think he ever will."

"Men should never completely step away from being boys. When they do, they lose the capacity to dream dreams that can change their worlds and the worlds of all those around them." Nanny finally took the seat beside the bed. She laced her fingers through Rohan's without disturbing the medical equipment.

"If they at least learned to pick up after themselves, it would be an improvement."

Despite the heavy emotions trapped in the room, Nanny chuckled. "Ah, but that is part of what we must put up with in order to keep them as they are. If they were perfect, we'd have nothing to do."

For a moment, the silence stretched. "What was Rohan like as a child, Nanny?"

The old woman shook her head. "Oh, he was quite a handful, this one was. Always into something. I ended up raising him."

"He mentioned that several times. He loves you very much."

"I know. That didn't stop him from walking his own way, though. Too much of his mother in him for that." Nanny smiled. "That's partly my fault, of course. I was never quite the stay-at-home mother my daughter wanted."

"I can see how flying floatplanes and helicopters could have gotten in the way of that."

"They did. And there were any number of other adventures. I took her with me on several of them, and I think that was the root of the wanderlust that made her leave us and go out to see the world. She was a Peace Corps volunteer. Worked with Doctors Without Borders. You've heard of them."

"Yes. Medical experts that work in impoverished regions."

"Those people see a lot of bad things in the world. Sickness. War. Famine. Evil things. I lost her in West

Africa. A fever took her. I didn't even get to say goodbye. She was just…gone."

"I'm sorry."

Tears glittered in the old woman's eyes. "That's something you just never get used to. Losing someone." She took a breath and looked at Rohan. "Rohan was only fourteen years old when she died, though he barely knew his mother after she became a doctor and went off to see the world. She never spoke of his father. My daughter never told anyone his name. I think maybe he was a married man. There was talk of a professor at her university. These things happen to young women. In her own way, I'm not sure she ever recovered from that, either."

Molly sat quietly and listened. Outside, people talked and the world went on as usual, but inside, the past was alive again.

"Rohan missed his mother, but they'd never been close. Not close enough."

"But he had you."

Nanny nodded proudly. "He did have me. And I taught him to throw baseballs and fish and even to fight."

"Fight?" That surprised Molly.

Nanny looked up at her and laughed. "I know. It seems far-fetched. Someone as small as me. But I learned how to fight because I grew up in a household with seven sisters and four brothers. You learn to scuffle in a large family."

Molly smiled.

"Should have maybe been my husband teaching Rohan." Nanny turned back to her grandson. "Would have been if Mose had lived. I lost him in a shipwreck during a storm. He worked with the coast guard."

So much misery. Molly didn't know what to say.

"Me and this one, we were always close. Always together. I made him grow up straight and tall as I could, but boys tend to have minds of their own."

"What is he doing in Blackpool? You mentioned that he didn't just end up here."

"He didn't. Something special brought him to this place."

"What?"

Nanny smoothed Rohan's forehead. "I don't know for sure yet. We'll have to figure that out. But I'm sure it had to do with the legend."

"The one about Charles Crowe and his hidden treasure?"

"That might be part of it, but there's more to it. You see, when Rohan was a child, I told him stories of the heritage we lost in West Africa during the slaving years. So many families got torn apart, and so much was lost. People were displaced, Molly, but heritage and culture?" Nanny shook her head. "That was all scattered and forgotten. I told Rohan that it was a wish of mine to see something of our family revealed. Our history. That was what he was doing here. And if he went to Aleister Crowe's home, it was because he believed that family has some of that history."

AFTER HE'D CONVINCED Paddington to talk with Nanny Myrie later, Michael left the inspector and went back into the hospital. He found Molly sitting with Nanny Myrie and Rohan. The old woman sat at her grandson's side and softly hummed to herself. Before he could enter, Molly waved him off.

Molly got up. "Nanny?"

The old woman looked up at her.

"I'm going to step outside for a cup of tea. Would you like anything?"

"Water would be fine."

"I'll be right back."

Nanny returned her attention to Rohan.

Outside the room, Molly took Michael by the arm. He kissed her forehead. "I guess I'm buying you a cup of tea."

"You are."

AT THE TEA SERVICE IN the waiting room, Molly looked at Michael. "You're certain you're all right?" She pulled at his shirt where the dead man's blood—and his own, though he'd never tell her—had dried.

"I'm fine." Michael poured tea and handed her a cup. "So what are we doing out here? I would have been glad to bring you a cup of tea."

"I wanted to talk to you away from Nanny. That poor woman is already carrying enough of a burden without hearing about everything that happened out there."

Michael sighed. "She's going to end up hearing about it, anyway."

"Why?"

"Because Dunkirk was visiting Rohan shortly before he was shot. I chased him out of the building." Michael quickly related the story and brought Molly up to speed.

"This man, Dunkirk—"

"Or whatever his name actually proves to be."

"—was working at the marina?"

"Yes."

"On one of the restoration projects that I brought to Blackpool?"

"It appears so."

Molly withdrew and wrapped her arms around herself.

"Hey." Michael took her hand in his. "That man didn't come to Blackpool to work on the marina. He came to break into Crowe's Nest. If he hadn't had the renovation to use as a cover, he'd have found something else. This isn't any fault of yours."

"Doesn't feel that way."

"If Rohan hadn't gone to Crowe's Nest, probably with this man, and Nanny Myrie wasn't sitting in that hospital room right now, would you feel this way?"

Molly let out a slow breath. "No. She's a good woman, Michael. She's been through a lot."

"I understand. I like Rohan." Michael shrugged and smiled. "We're not going to give up on them. We're going to help them. But we can't do that by dwelling on the past."

"The past seems to be where all this started. You said you never knew why Rohan came here?"

Michael shook his head. "When we first met he told me he was just passing through. Looking for work."

"But he spent a lot of time with you."

"Blame my magnetic personality."

"Oh, I blame you for many things, Michael Graham. And you can, under the right conditions, have an inflated view of yourself."

"Ouch. Did I tell you I was very nearly shot today?"

"You said the sniper deliberately missed you." Molly fisted his shirt and pulled him close. She kissed him and the chemistry that bound them sizzled anew inside Michael's body. She pulled away entirely too soon. "For which I'm eternally grateful. What I want you to focus on is that Rohan made sure he was with you, and the two of you were always working on those models of the town buildings."

Michael thought about that, remembering how Rohan had been interested in his extracurricular project practically from the moment he'd heard about it. "Funny, I never noticed that before."

"Because you were so caught up in figuring out how the model fit together. You become quite distracted when you're trying to figure something out."

"Possibly."

"Definitely. The point is, you were blind to Rohan's interest."

Michael looked at her and realized there was something she wasn't telling him. "You know why Rohan is here."

"Nanny Myrie says that Rohan came here searching for possible artifacts that were taken during the slave trade. She thinks Rohan connected the artifacts to the Crowe family."

"But how? Blackpool was long associated with smuggling, but evidence of slave trading was only found recently with the discovery of the *Seaclipse*. And there is no evidence tying the Crowe family to it."

"Maybe we should ask Nanny."

"Speaking of Nanny, Paddington would like to have a meeting with her, as well." Michael glanced around. "I don't really think this place would be good for that."

"I won't have her taken to the Blackpool police station and questioned there."

"She could choose not to go."

Molly gave him a look. "Do you really suppose Paddington is going to let that stop him?"

"No. Not with that dead man out there and still no answers about what's going on."

"I have a simple solution."

"All ears, love."

"Ask the inspector to dinner with us tonight. He can talk to Nanny there."

"Under our watchful eye?"

"Of course."

"I don't think Paddington will have a problem with that. He'll get a good meal thrown in."

"I'll call Iris and have her see about dinner arrangements." Molly took out her mobile.

"You do that and I'll go meet Rohan's grandmother." Michael turned and started to walk away.

"Wait." Molly paid for one of the bottles of water from the vending machine and handed it over to Michael. "She wanted water."

BACK AT ROHAN'S ROOM, Michael introduced himself and handed Nanny Myrie the bottled water.

"Thank you, Mr. Graham."

"You're welcome. Please, call me Michael."

"Michael." The old woman drank. "My grandson thinks a lot of you."

"I wasn't aware you'd been in touch."

"An email from the internet café here and there. Not much. But he did mention the model you two were building of the town. He said you thought it was more than just a model."

"Yes—it's a puzzle of some sort. The buildings actually fit together to form a three-dimensional object, but I don't know what its purpose is. Maybe it has to do with the tunnels underneath the buildings…. Rohan improved a lot of the buildings. If it hadn't been for his skill, I don't think I would've realized it was a puzzle."

Someone cleared his voice.

Looking up, Michael saw Lockwood Nightingale standing in the doorway. The guard Paddington had assigned to the room had the solicitor out for the moment, but Nightingale didn't seem as if he was going to be easily dissuaded.

CHAPTER SEVEN

"MRS. MYRIE, MY NAME IS Lockwood Nightingale. I need to have a word with you."

Michael faced the man and took one step, enough to put himself between Nightingale and Rohan's grandmother. "Perhaps this isn't the right time."

The solicitor stood his ground. "Mr. Graham, although I can see no reason for this to be any of your concern, perhaps you can suggest a better opportunity for a discussion between Mrs. Myrie and myself."

"I can't say." Michael kept his voice calm but it was sheathed in steel. There was something about the man's elitist attitude that rubbed him the wrong way. Getting money or being born into money just didn't agree with some people. "But *this* is definitely not the time or the place."

Nightingale peered past Michael at the old woman. "We could let Mrs. Myrie speak for herself."

"About what?" Nanny stood and approached, but she didn't step past Michael's side.

"I represent Mr. Aleister Crowe, Mrs. Myrie."

"The man that put my grandson in that bed?"

Nightingale froze for just a moment, but he didn't bat an eye. "Quite."

Nanny's face turned hard. "Is Mr. Crowe too afraid to speak to me himself?"

"I advised him not to."

"Why would you do that?"

"I thought it wouldn't be prudent."

"So you're protecting him."

Michael had to work to keep a grin off his face. Apparently Rohan's grandmother didn't take nonsense from slick solicitors.

"I wouldn't say that I was protecting him, Mrs. Myrie."

"Let me say it for you." Nanny crossed her arms and regarded Nightingale as though he were something repugnant.

"There are legal matters that need attending to. I thought perhaps we might address them. I am in a position to ensure that Mr. Crowe is not interested in bringing criminal charges against your grandson in return for an agreement that your grandson won't pursue a civil matter regarding the shooting."

"Mr. Nightingale, was it?"

Nightingale nodded, and he preened just a little. Obviously he liked the sound of his own name.

"For the record, and you can quote me on this, there is *nothing* civil about shooting an unarmed man." Nanny's voice was as harsh as a whipcrack.

The burly policeman standing at the door chuckled, then covered the noise with a cough.

Nightingale glared at the man but didn't say anything. He swiveled his attention back to Nanny with laser intensity. "Before you insist on making anything personal of this, you might want to consider your grandson's future. If he comes out of that coma—"

"*When* he comes out of the coma."

"—do you really want him spending the next several years in prison for breaking and entering?"

"Mr. Nightingale, I may look like an old woman to you, and my grandson may look like he's on his deathbed, but that's not the case. I'm not a stupid person and Rohan hasn't stopped fighting. I know that Mr. Aleister Crowe can't stop a criminal court from pressing charges if it wishes to, and my grandson's fate was decided the moment he stepped into that house. You have nothing to offer me. You only want me to release your employer."

Nightingale sniffed at that. "Aleister isn't my employer. He's my friend."

"You'll excuse me my rudeness due to my age, which you've already sought to take advantage of, but I know an employee when I see one. You *work* for people, Mr. Nightingale. No matter how much money you make and how much of a rich veneer you put on, that's not going to change. You think like an employee."

Nightingale flushed red.

"Please don't contact me in the future, Mr. Nightingale. I will definitely be far less cordial than I am today. If you need to get in touch with me regarding legal matters, I'll have my attorney contact you."

"Do you have a solicitor?" Nightingale struggled to save face.

"I'm sure Mr. Graham can help me sort one out."

Michael smiled. "It would be my pleasure."

"Mrs. Myrie—"

The policeman turned toward Nightingale. "Sir, the lady has been very polite, in my opinion, and it's my opinion that matters here. Now, she's gently told you to shove off, so I'd be for shoving off if I was you. Otherwise I might be inclined to point out she could file a harassment complaint and have you carried down to the police station."

Nightingale didn't say anything further, but he fired one of his engraved business cards into the air.

Eyes and hands trained by thousands of hours of gaming, Michael plucked the card from the air and made the feat look effortless. "We'll be in touch, Mr. Nightingale."

The solicitor strode away.

Nanny patted the policeman on the arm. "Thank you, Officer."

The man smiled and winked at her. "It was my pleasure, madam. I don't care for a puffed-up popinjay like that one. And you've enough troubles without him adding to them."

Taking Michael by the arm, Nanny turned him around and walked back to the bed. "Michael, I know that you might believe I'm a frail old woman—"

"Actually, Nanny, I stand corrected."

"Good. I'm glad that we've got that out of the way." Nanny stopped at the bed. "I know Inspector Paddington will wish to speak with me."

"He's already mentioned that."

"The quicker we get that over with, the better. That way, the inspector can mark that off his to-do list and move on to whatever else he has on his plate. We need him out of the way."

"We do?"

"Perhaps that was presumptuous of me. I hope to find out more about what drove Rohan to invade the Crowe house that night. He wouldn't have gone there unless he had a reason."

"I agree."

"Then I'll need to start looking for those answers."

"I'd love to help."

"*We'd* love to help," Molly said as she walked through the doorway to the room. "No one else I know can keep Michael out of trouble."

Nanny smiled at that. "I'm sure you can't keep him completely out of trouble."

"Perhaps not." Molly smiled ruefully. "But no one does it better."

"I would rather not meet the inspector on his home territory, either," Nanny continued. "Somewhere away from the police department, I should think. And away from prying eyes."

"You know, I believe I have just the place."

Nanny's eyes twinkled. "I'm not surprised."

"How about dinner at our house?"

"Home-court rules?"

"Of course."

Michael shook his head in amazement. Nanny Myrie and Molly had already stepped in sync. Paddington had no idea what he was in for.

"MOLLY, I CAN GET A ROOM in one of the bed-and-breakfasts in Blackpool. Please don't go to any trouble for me."

Leading the way up to the second-floor guest room, Molly shook her head. "Actually, you wouldn't be able to. With all the construction going on in Blackpool, housing has become a bit of a problem." She opened the door to the bedroom.

Nanny stepped into the room and gazed around. "Oh my, this is marvelous."

Molly knew that and took pride in it. Thorne-Shower

Mansion had a long history in the community. She and Michael had been excited to purchase the home and had done it over according to their tastes without losing any of the original charm. A four-poster bed occupied the room with a vanity, wardrobe, small table and chairs and a recliner. Molly had redone the room in sea-foam green and accented it with shells.

"Michael insisted on setting up an entertainment center." Molly opened the unit's doors to reveal a large plasma screen. "You've got more TV channels here than you'll find at any bed-and-breakfast in town, and movies are also available."

"I doubt there will be much time for television."

"But if there is, you're fixed up." Molly opened the door to the bathroom. "This is one of the rooms with a full bath. And you'll find extra towels and blankets here." She pointed to the small linen closet. "If you need anything else, please don't hesitate to ask. Michael and I both want your stay with us to be as comfortable as possible."

"Thank you for this, Molly." Nanny hugged her.

"It's my pleasure. I'm sure Michael and Irwin will be up with your bags shortly. Now, if you're set, I'm going to help Iris in the kitchen."

"Give me just a few minutes to freshen up and I'll join you."

"You don't have to do that."

"Nonsense." Nanny waved away any objections. "Give me something to do with my hands, child. Otherwise I'll worry myself to death."

"All right. I'll see you in a little while." Molly left the room and closed the door behind her. She wondered if she would have the same kind of fortitude to see things through if she faced all that the older woman did. Then she realized that Nanny didn't have a choice.

MICHAEL ENTERED THE KITCHEN, headed for the large side-by-side refrigerator and took out a beer. He twisted the cap off and expertly fired it into the trash bin. He drank and looked out into the spacious backyard.

"Hello, Michael." Iris Dunstead stood at one of the islands in the center of the room and sliced vegetables with staccato precision. She was a thin, dapper woman in her early seventies. She wore her white hair short and tonight sported a cook's apron over a deep green dress.

"Hello, Iris. The slave driver isn't around?"

"I heard that." Molly stepped out of the walk-in cooler with attached freezer. Someone in Thorne-Shower's past had loved to entertain and had installed the huge units and kitchen area. Molly carried a tray of marinated steaks.

"Well, you weren't meant to."

"As punishment, you're going to cook the meat."

"And if I'd quietly drunk my beer instead of making that comment?"

"Oh, you'd still have cooked the meat."

Mrs. Dunstead laughed.

Molly handed Michael the tray of steaks and lightly kissed him. "Make certain you feel properly guilty. Nanny and I decided we wanted to help Iris in the kitchen instead of waiting around with nothing to do."

"And you decided I needed something to do, as well."

"I did."

"Any particular way you want these prepared?"

Michael smelled the lime juice, garlic, oregano, cumin and chipotle peppers in the marinade. "Adobo?"

"Adobo."

"They're going to cook fast once I get started."

"I'll let you know when." Molly removed a bunch of salad ingredients from the refrigerator and closed the door with her hip. "You'll at least have time to finish your beer."

"You're a love, Mrs. Graham. Truly you are." Michael plopped down at the small breakfast table in the corner and took another sip of his beer.

"You got the rest of Nanny's things carried upstairs?" Molly split a lettuce head with a practiced swipe of a knife.

"Yes. The way that woman stood up to Lockwood Nightingale was impressive, but I was even more impressed with her packing. You would have taken at least three times as many bags if we were going anywhere."

Molly stopped what she was doing and pointed the knife at him. "You do realize I'm armed?"

"I blame the weather. It's got me off my game."

Molly returned to her task. "Inspector Paddington?"

"Will be here as requested."

"Good. Did he have any problems with the arrangement?"

"Not once he realized no other arrangements were forthcoming. After that, I think he cozied up to the idea of a free dinner."

"An elegant dinner."

"Once I perfectly cook these steaks, I'm sure that's what it will be."

"Is there a humble bone in your body, Michael Graham?"

"Of course there is. I haven't misplaced it." Michael opened a file on his iPhone and pulled up images of the 3D model he'd put together of Blackpool as it had been when Charles Crowe, Aleister's ancestor, had lived.

The doorbell rang.

Michael flicked through the programs available on his mobile and pulled up a security-camera view of the main gates. Inspector Paddington's small car sat there. "Well, the inspector has arrived."

"Let him in. When you get back, we'll be finishing up and you can put the steaks on."

"Sure. Just don't let him do too much talking to Nanny when I'm not here."

Michael opened the audio connection to the front gates. "Good evening, Inspector. Won't you drive ahead? I'll meet you outside." He tapped the security button that opened the gates.

In response Paddington said, "We found out who the dead man really was."

Before Michael could ask the obvious question, Paddington engaged his car's transmission and drove up.

Michael glanced out the window and watched the inspector's car follow the winding road to the main house. "Apparently Inspector Paddington is developing a sense of the theatrical, as well."

Molly frowned. "Or he wants to see how we react when we hear the news."

Iris raised an eyebrow. "If it's too bad, we can always withhold dessert."

CHAPTER EIGHT

INSPECTOR PADDINGTON GOT OUT of his car. "Am I early?"

"Only a few minutes. We've got one other guest coming." Michael waited on the porch.

"Anyone I know?"

"Professor Algernon Hume-Thorson."

Algernon was the lead in the recovery of the *Seaclipse*. The affable professor had proven himself likable, even to Paddington and his grumpy ways.

"Any special reason the professor has been invited out?"

"Molly's idea."

Paddington grunted and climbed the steps. He carried a thin nine-by-twelve-inch manila envelope. "Some of the things we'll be discussing tonight might be better to stay among us."

"I trust Algernon. He's the soul of discretion when it comes to anything that isn't old news." Michael smiled.

"We'll see."

"Since you're early, how about I set you up with a pint? I'm having one in the kitchen."

"Sure."

MICHAEL HELD UP A CORKED BOTTLE of beer and a stein. "You'll want a glass with this."

"I never drink beer in a glass unless it's served that way." Taking the bottle, Paddington squinted at the label.

"Gale's Prize Old Ale."

"Never had the pleasure."

"It's a pleasure, Inspector. Trust me. It was made by George Gale and Company, Limited, in Hordean, Hampshire. This isn't a beer that you drink young. It has to be aged at least a few years before you open it up. I've put several bottles of this back in the cellar."

Staring at the bottle doubtfully, Paddington pushed aside the manila envelope he'd brought and put the stein on the table. He took the corkscrew Michael gave him and gently opened the beer. Once it was open, he sniffed speculatively, then looked up. "Smells like rotting wood that's gone sour." He sniffed again. "Maybe a hint of vanilla?"

"Maybe." Michael opened his own beer. "The nose of this particular beer seems to strike people differently."

Carefully, Paddington filled the stein. The ale rose up the color of mahogany and gave a thin tan head. He took a sip, sloshed it around, then swallowed. "That's good."

"Doesn't take you long to become a believer."

"I know my ales."

Nanny Myrie, attired in more casual clothing, entered the kitchen. When he saw her, Inspector Paddington got to his feet.

Michael stood, as well. "Mrs. Myrie, allow me to introduce Inspector Paddington, Blackpool's top policeman."

Nanny walked over and offered her hand. "Inspector."

"Madam."

"I'm glad you could join us here."

"With the offer of dinner and an exceptionally fine ale, how could I refuse?"

Nanny smiled. "Would it be possible to shelve conversation about my grandson and those unfortunate circumstances till after dinner?"

Paddington hesitated only a moment. "Of course."

"Thank you." Nanny turned her attention to Molly and Iris. "Ladies, what can I do to help you?"

Michael sat and picked up his ale. The beer was a favorite of his. He eyed the manila envelope.

Following Michael's gaze, Paddington slid the envelope off the table and onto the chair with him. "After dinner. Didn't you hear?" He smiled.

"Enjoying your little game, Inspector?"

"I think it's only fair that occasionally the shoe slips onto the other foot."

"Michael?" Molly called. "Can you put the steaks on now?"

With a last look at the inspector, Michael stood and went to start grilling.

"—AND THERE I WAS, face-to-face with this bloody great white shark, and only a few minutes of air and a panicked marine photojournalist for company." Algernon Hume-Thorson lounged in his chair at the dinner table with a stein of Gale's in one hand. He was a natural, professional and polished storyteller, a man who could walk into a drawing room or a bar and slowly draw the attention of everyone in the room.

In his mid-thirties, Algernon didn't look the way Molly had first imagined him when Arliss Hogan had offered to call him in to look at the shipwreck. She'd pictured a man with a salt-and-pepper beard, glasses and a pipe. Algernon was smooth-shaven, tanned and had bright blue eyes. He wore an obnoxious Hawaiian shirt that could have been featured on an episode of *Magnum, P.I.,* white Dockers pants and sandals. He was completely at ease with who he was.

Algernon was as trim and fit as Michael, and tended to be just as physical on the soccer or rugby field. Molly had watched the professor and her husband compete with a fierceness that bordered on frightening. Yet they accepted each other as equals and never walked off the playing field with unresolved grudges—no matter how bloodied and battered they were.

That physical relationship, so similar to the one that Michael enjoyed with Rohan, was something Molly understood but couldn't quite grasp. It had something to do with a nuance of masculinity that escaped her.

Even now, Michael hung on the professor's words, caught up in the tale like a five-year-old. Nanny and Iris listened attentively, certain of the outcome because Algernon sat before them, while Inspector Paddington and Irwin sat patiently awaiting the punch line. Molly loved watching Michael when he acted like this. That irrepressible zest for life and belief in heroes and adventure were the things that had first drawn her to him. Her business was about dreams, as well, but they were more rooted in everyday life than Michael's.

Algernon sipped his beer, enjoying Michael's impatience.

Michael couldn't wait any longer. "So what did you do?"

"I grabbed the photojournalist—Marty, I think his

name was—and yanked him back inside the wreck with me." Algernon put his beer down and leaned forward across the table, focusing entirely on Michael now.

Unconsciously, Michael leaned across the table, too, drawn to the man and his tale. Molly almost laughed but restrained herself because she knew it would break the spell Algernon had so skillfully woven.

"That great white came after us like a lightning bolt. Bam!" He slapped the tabletop with his open palm. "I swear, I've never seen anything move so fast in my life. I kept swimming, and I truly expected to only be hauling a piece of Marty along after me for all my troubles. But I'd snatched him out of the jaws of death. Later, he told me that himself."

"What did the shark do?"

"That ungainly brute swam right through the hole in the side of the ship and went for us. I swam through the ship's hold and used crates for cover, only to watch irreplaceable artifacts destroyed in a heartbeat. It was hard, I'll have you know, and I thought how callous it was of me to go inside the ship when I could have just as easily stayed outside."

"You wouldn't have escaped."

"At the time, I didn't think Marty and I were going to escape, anyway. Better to die outside and leave the site unharmed than to make a mess of things."

"You didn't really think that!" In his own way, the inspector had gotten drawn in, as well.

Algernon shifted his attention to Paddington. "Inspector, if you were in a potentially lethal altercation and you had a choice about ruining a crime scene, would you hesitate?"

Paddington drummed his fingers on the tabletop. "I see your point, Professor. It is a quandary."

"The great white." Michael shifted in his chair.

"Right." Algernon focused on him. "So we were in the hold, swimming for our very lives, and the sea's cruelest killer is right at our stern. Escape seemed impossible. I swear, that's the closest I've ever been to death. But I was thinking the whole time. You can't do what I do and not learn to use everything around you."

Molly knew Michael's brain was racing, because this was exactly the kind of scenario that he would dream up for a video game.

"Then I thought of Marty's camera." Algernon grinned. "More precisely, I thought of his light—a high-powered high-pressure sodium light."

Michael smiled then. "Nice." He sat back in his chair, satisfied with the answer he had come up with on his own.

"What?" Paddington was a little miffed because he'd missed something.

Molly felt the same way.

"Did you flash the shark with the light and scare it away?" she asked.

"Not exactly."

Michael leaned forward again. "Let me see if I've got this right."

Algernon waved acceptance, giving Michael the floor, and took another sip of his ale.

"The camera used a high-pressure sodium bulb. I'm sure Marty had spares."

"He did indeed." Algernon grinned and nodded. "Very good, Michael."

"I don't understand." Molly held up a hand. "Some of us didn't live for science class."

"Then you missed out on lessons that could one day save your life." Michael winked at her. "What do you know about sodium, love?"

"Combine it with chloride and you have table salt." Molly held up a silver saltshaker.

"True. Which is one of the most common forms for sodium, by the way. The Egyptians had something similar called natron—a natural mineral salt containing hydrated sodium carbonate—and used it to embalm mummies. Pure sodium wasn't successfully separated into an unadulterated state until the early nineteenth century."

Paddington heaved a sigh. "Mr. Wizard. Don't know how you put up with him, Mrs. Graham."

"He does sometimes live in rarified air."

Michael ignored the comments. "The thing about sodium, and all the other alkali metals on the periodic chart, is that they react with water."

"React how?"

"They burn. That's why fire-suppression teams have to deal with metal fires differently than common fires. The addition of water in metal fires will actually make things worse." Michael turned back to Algernon. "I take it you made things worse for the great white."

"I pulled my knife, cut the straps on Marty's equipment bag, knowing he carried spare bulbs for his camera, and waited for the shark to strike. When it did, I pushed the equipment bag into its face. The shark chewed on the bag for a moment, savaging it to the point that I thought my ill-conceived plan wasn't going to save us. But, finally, the thing bit into one of those bulbs. The bulbs were designed to withstand pressure down a few thousand meters, but they weren't tested against the bite of a great white. When the beast broke one of the bulbs, it suddenly had a mouthful of fire." Algernon gestured with his empty stein. "Naturally, the shark turned tail and swam off. Thankfully I never saw it again."

Michael sat back in his chair with a thoughtful expression. "You know, I may steal that scenario. You can't just tell something like that to a game designer and not have him lift it off you straightaway, mate."

Algernon laughed good-naturedly. "Feel free. That story has paid for a lot of beer all over the world for me."

"Speaking of stories, perhaps we could get to this evening's agenda." Paddington placed the manila envelope on the table. "If we're all ready."

Nanny Myrie sat up straighter. "I think it's time."

"Let me get a bottle of the good brandy." Iris excused herself from the table. Molly started to get up, but the older woman waved her back into her seat.

"If I may, Mrs. Myrie." Paddington fished out a notepad from inside his jacket.

"Of course."

"Do you know why your grandson came to Blackpool?"

"I do." Nanny cleared her throat. "My people have carried stories down from the Before Times—"

"Excuse me?"

"From the time before my people were brought from West Africa and delivered to the New World as slaves and chattel. The way some of my ancestors tell it, our forebears were leaders of my people."

"What people?"

"The Yoruba people. They lived in the lower western Niger area. For long and long, it is said, the Oya Empire guided our people. Our ways spread to many places."

Algernon nodded. "Historians have traced Yoruba influences to Cuba, Brazil and Haiti. Their practices, some believe, paved the way for Santeria, Voudoun and Candomble."

"Voodoo?" Paddington tapped his pen irritably. "Begging your pardon, Mrs. Myrie, but I don't want to go filling my reports with mentions of voodoo."

"Detective Inspector, I never mentioned voodoo. I only said that my people have a long and important history. That is what Rohan was here to save."

"How?"

"Our people were enslaved by other tribes. My ancestors stood on the slave blocks in Île de Gorée and got sold into servitude. Their possessions were taken from them by their captors and by the European sailors that chained them in the bowels of their ships. The stories my family have handed down talk of some of these objects that were stolen. If you care to search further on the matter, you'll find that exhaustive studies have been done on the Yoruba people."

"That's true, Inspector." Algernon narrowed his eyes and thought. "There are, in fact, some researchers that believe the Yoruba people might have been the fabled Atlanteans. There's evidence that the Yoruba sailed the Atlantic and discovered the New World before the Europeans did. They were shipbuilders and traders, and there's some speculation that part of West Africa sank into the ocean, just like Atlantis did, at around the time those stories started."

Paddington held up his hands in surrender. "Stop. Let's go forward a few hundred years."

"More like a few thousand."

"All right." Paddington took a breath and showed restraint. Molly knew it was hard for the man to remain patient under the circumstances. Especially with a body in the Blackpool morgue that he still couldn't explain. "Let's get back to the here and now. To just a few nights ago, in fact. Why was your grandson in the Crowes' house, Mrs. Myrie?"

Iris returned with the brandy and glasses. She poured quietly and passed the drinks around to everyone except Nanny and Irwin, both of whom politely declined.

"Charles Crowe was reputed to be quite a collector. He founded the museum in Blackpool, but rumor has it he kept all the choice pieces for himself. My grandson believed the Crowes still had some of our stolen artifacts. Objects Charles Crowe likely obtained from being part of the slave trade."

CHAPTER NINE

THE REVELATION STUNNED MOLLY, and she knew it set Michael back, as well. He didn't have any questions. He just sat there and stared at Nanny Myrie in fascination.

"Playing the devil's advocate, Mrs. Myrie, and meaning no disrespect, but can you prove that?" Paddington tapped his pen against his notebook irritably. He was obviously unaware of the action.

"I can." Nanny reached down beside her chair and pulled up her purse. She rummaged in it for a moment, then produced a much-folded envelope and an ancient journal. She opened the envelope and spread photographs and old newspaper articles across the table.

"May I?" Michael pointed to the pictures.

Nanny nodded. "Please. Help yourselves. These are only copies. I have the originals Rohan sent me at home."

Algernon dug into the photographs, as well, plucking out a couple and surveying them. He studied them for a long moment.

Molly took the newspaper article Nanny offered her. It featured a picture of a pair of primitive male figures with elongated heads standing side by side on a shelf behind a glass pane. "The article says these artifacts were being exhibited at the Blackpool Maritime Museum, on loan from the Crowe estate."

"Yes, though they've since been removed. I can only assume Rohan went to Crowe's Nest to find them. Those figures are very important to my culture."

"Why?"

"They are *ibeji*. Twins."

"Here's another interesting fact about the Yoruba people." Algernon glanced over the tops of the pages he held. "Twins run in high numbers in their culture. Not monozygotic twins, mind you, but dizygotic twins."

"God help me." Paddington looked beaten. "In English, if you please, Professor."

Algernon shrugged. "Sorry. Monozygotic twins are identical, from the same egg. Dizygotic twins are fraternal, from different eggs."

"You could have simply said that."

Ignoring the inspector, Algernon watched Nanny. "While the number of identical twins are about the same throughout the world, usually around four births in a thousand, the number of fraternal twins is about forty-five births in a thousand in the Yoruba culture. In fact, there is one city—I cannot for the life of me remember the name—that clocks in with twin births at about one hundred and fifty per thousand."

"Why are their numbers so different?" Irwin looked puzzled.

Algernon shrugged. "No one knows."

"Twins are a part of my family's heritage, as well." Nanny looked at the photographs on the table. "I was a twin, though my sister died early in our lives. And Rohan was born a twin, though his brother passed away before the new day dawned." She shook her head. "My grandson felt the pressure of having to live two lives, to have to be twice as successful so that he might honor his brother's memory. He always said that his brother lingered in the spirit world and helped to guide him. And perhaps that's true. Rohan is finding the strength somehow to stay alive."

Paddington looked apoplectic and Molly couldn't help feeling sorry for the man. The interview was going everywhere but where he had thought it would.

"Please." Paddington raised his hands. "For the sake of brevity, let's assume those statues of twins are in Crowe's Nest."

"My grandson risked everything because he was sure they are."

"But how can you prove they have anything to do with your family history?"

Nanny opened the journal to a place marked with a ribbon. "This book belonged to my great-grandfather. He started it after he reached the New World. He was taken as a boy from his homeland and didn't know how to write in his native tongue. That was one of the things immediately lost to him. He learned, illegally, to write in English while living in Jamaica. This was during a time when a slave learning such a thing was punishable by death."

Placing the journal on the table, Nanny revealed the relevant pages. On the left was a drawing of the *ibeji*. "My ancestor writes here of the loss of the statues. The names of all the family leaders, from the first to the last, were written on them. They were something his family had saved from the slavers. But the statues were found in Île de Gorée."

Paddington sighed in resignation. "I'm going to regret asking, but what is Île de Gorée?"

"It is an island, Inspector, and part of the outlying area

of Dakar, Senegal, at present." Nanny's voice sounded hoarse and Molly knew that she was tired from her long flight and the emotional stress she was under. "More slaves were sold at other ports. From Saint-Louis or Gambia. But my ancestors were sold in Île de Gorée. I could walk that island—though I have never seen it—because I have learned much about it, and I shared that knowledge with Rohan. I filled that boy's head with all these stories from the day he was born. So, you see, if anyone put him in that house that night, it was me."

"That's not true, madam," Paddington insisted, "so let me lift that burden from you. I'll get to that in a moment." He tapped the picture of the *ibeji*. "You can't tell me the statues are the same ones your ancestor wrote about."

Nanny never flinched. "Look at their hands, Inspector Paddington. One of them is missing a right hand."

Molly examined the photograph she held and saw that was true. She hadn't noticed it earlier.

Quietly, Nanny pushed the journal out into the center of the table again. "Now look at this."

Studying the inked drawing on the page, Molly saw that one of those statues was also missing a right hand.

"My great-grandfather drew this image on January 14, 1829."

Paddington sighed and pinched the bridge of his nose. "There's no way you can prove that drawing was made in 1829."

"I disagree." Algernon's voice was gentle, but his rebuke was immediate. "That journal and those pages can definitely be dated. Now we're in my bailiwick, Inspector."

Paddington drew a breath. "All right. For the time being, let's say those statues are the same ones exhibited in the museum. Why did your grandson think he could find them at Crowe's Nest?"

Nanny clasped her hands calmly. "I'm not sure. All he told me was that he wanted to find out what else Charles Crowe had taken from our family and our people."

"Other than his reputation as a collector, what proof is there that Charles Crowe had anything to do with this?"

"The article says the museum loaned the artifacts from the Crowe, and Charles Crowe is named in this book." Nanny turned a few pages. When she opened the journal again and shoved it out for everyone to see, the likeness of one man's features was sharp and clear despite the yellowing pages. Underneath the head shot, *Charles Crowe* was written in a fine, neat hand.

Without a word, Michael got out his iPhone, punched in a few entries, then placed the mobile down on the table beside the journal. "That's Charles Crowe. I took a photo of the man's portrait that hangs inside the Blackpool Library."

The resemblance was unmistakable.

MICHAEL STARED AT THE TWO images on the table and felt flummoxed. He hadn't had a clue what Rohan had been chasing the whole time he'd been in Blackpool. Michael was also somewhat disenchanted with Paddington's attitude. He felt the inspector should be more excited about everything they were finding out. When he glanced at Molly, he could tell from her slightly irritated expression that she was thinking the same thing.

"You believe your grandson went to Crowe's Nest

that night to do what?" Paddington focused on Nanny Myrie. "If he was so bent on recovering artifacts taken from your family, why didn't he lodge a complaint?"

"According to my ancestor's journal, Charles Crowe was an avid collector of tribal art and items with curses. Molly mentioned there was some trouble with Charles Crowe and a gypsy family named Draghici, as well. All of these things are tied into Charles Crowe's treasure hoard."

"If that exists." Paddington didn't look pleased.

Michael couldn't blame the inspector. Stefan Draghici and his lot had cast a dark shadow over the community ever since they'd appeared in town.

"And that attitude is why Rohan didn't want to lodge a complaint without proof that the treasure existed. I can't speak to the gypsy gold, but these relics *do* exist," Nanny said. "And they need to be returned to their rightful owners." She flipped the pages. "My ancestor mentions several other things that were taken from the prisoners. Rohan hoped to find any pieces that hadn't been donated to museums in Charles Crowe's name. Getting donated items back would have proven difficult, maybe impossible. But Rohan believed that if he could find Crowe's treasure trove, we would stand a better chance of getting our own artifacts back. But it wasn't just about us. He wanted those things returned to *all* the rightful owners."

"Owning the property of slaves would have been awkward for Charles Crowe." Michael stared down at the image on his mobile. "Given that participating in the slavery business was illegal in England at the time, Charles Crowe would have faced heavy fines and prison time."

"That's why he must have ordered Jeremy Chatwhistle killed." Algernon sipped his beer.

"Jeremy Chatwhistle, the skeleton we found in the underground tunnels while we were trying to find the murderer of Willie Myners?"

"Oh." The professor looked embarrassed. "Sorry. We've been so busy talking about these things that I forgot to mention that I heard from a marine-archivist friend of mine today. He managed to find several of Chatwhistle's reports to his superiors and interesting references in the good captain's journals."

"What did they say?" Michael waited anxiously.

"Captain Chatwhistle was posted to the West Africa squadron, and was commended several times for his determination and success at catching slave traders. But his commanders at the Royal Navy were unhappy about his pursuit of one particular ship—the *Seaclipse*—all the way from Africa to English waters. He begged them for more time, saying he was close to interdicting the ship and arresting its captain, and its owner—Charles Crowe." He paused. "Obviously Charles Crowe or his men found Chatwhistle first. And the Royal Navy dropped the issue."

For a moment, silence hung around the table.

"All right, then." Paddington sat forward. "I've listened to all of you put forth all kinds of summations. Now it's time we have mine." He cleared his throat. "I think that, given what you've told me here, your grandson had some altruistic reasons for being at Crowe's Nest the night he was shot, Mrs. Myrie. But that doesn't excuse him from breaking the law."

"I didn't expect that it would."

"It doesn't excuse Mr. Crowe from shooting him that

night, either, but that would be something for the courts to decide. If it ever comes to that. It's my belief that no criminal charges will be filed against Aleister Crowe."

"Why?"

"Mr. Crowe is well connected and I have been advised that filing charges for shooting an intruder in his own home would not be approved of by my superiors." Paddington colored a little, but Michael didn't know if that was from anger or embarrassment. "At any rate, I believe that your grandson could have been *coerced* into following his altruistic instincts a mite more actively than he might have done on his own."

"You don't think Rohan acted alone?"

"Not to take anything away from your grandson, madam, although this does and you should be thankful for it, I've found nothing in his background that suggests he would be skilled enough to breach Mr. Crowe's security measures. You see, that has been a conundrum for me since I first learned of the matter. The man Mr. Graham accosted today has shed more light on the subject."

Deftly, Paddington opened his manila envelope and extracted a mug shot. Michael recognized the face immediately as the murdered man at the hospital.

"Dunkirk?" Michael studied the harsh features.

"Not anymore. Meet Mr. Timothy Harper. A bloke who knows the inner workings of security systems the way you know video games, Mr. Graham." Paddington pulled out more photographs and sheets of type-filled paper. "According to his jacket, Mr. Harper has been in and out of correctional institutions since he was knee-high. The detective I talked to in London Metro tells me that Mr. Harper was part of an efficient criminal ring. They specialize in taking down big scores."

"You think they were after the Crowe family?"

"I don't think they were after West African artifacts that the rest of the world has more or less forgotten." Paddington glanced at Nanny. "Meaning no disrespect, madam."

Nanny waved his words away. "What you're saying makes sense, Inspector, but you'll have to forgive me. I don't see my grandson taking up with people like this."

"He probably wasn't aware he was taking up with *people*." Michael scowled at Harper's picture. "He thought he was taking up with Dunkirk."

Paddington nodded. "I believe Harper got Rohan into Crowe's Nest that night, and I believe he left him there when he got shot."

"No honor among thieves." Algernon's voice was a low growl.

"Oh, karma is plainly a coldhearted harpy when it comes to that," Paddington said. "I believe one of Harper's partners blew him out of his socks today." Suddenly self-conscious, he glanced at the women. "Pardon my coarseness."

Michael sipped his brandy. "I don't suppose any of Harper's known crew is a sniper?"

"As a matter of fact, there are two men who are noted for their shooting abilities. One of them was an armorer for the army, and the other is an assassin. Either one is capable of making the shot that killed Harper."

Michael studied the photos of Harper's suspected gang affiliates. What had Rohan gotten himself into? What had he gotten them *all* into?

CHAPTER TEN

MICHAEL WOKE EARLY THE NEXT morning, put on a wireless headset and pushed the button that raised the huge plasma television from its recessed hiding place in the bedroom floor. Molly hadn't liked the idea of a television in the bedroom, but once it was out of sight, there was no evidence of modern technology. Even the lights were disguised as oil lanterns. Sleeping in the room was like sliding back into the past.

Despite Inspector Paddington's best effort to work with the press to get the story about the sniper shooting shut down, the news broke anyway. Considering the circumstances of the murder, the story was doomed to get an attentive audience. Too many ingredients to tempt popular curiosity.

A number of reporters who'd been in Blackpool to cover the marina makeover and the shipwreck suddenly decided that they wanted to use their cameras to do "real" news. It seemed that most of them had shown up at Merciful Angels Hospital the previous day. Michael was willing to bet that YouTube had been flooded with video spots concerning the murder.

Lying quietly in bed with Molly beside him, he remembered her mentioning the man who had been watching her at the marina when she'd gone to pick up Nanny Myrie, and it made him nervous. Evidently whoever had been watching Molly had already decided that she presented a danger or a source of information.

A hand lifted the earpiece of the headset. "Penny for your thoughts, love."

Startled, Michael looked over at Molly. "Did I wake you? I'm sorry."

"No, you didn't wake me. My offer for a glimpse into the thoughts of Michael Graham stands."

"Not much there, I'm afraid." He took in a breath and let it out. "I'm not getting a good feeling about what's going on. I don't like the fact that someone was tailing you at the same time Timothy Harper was getting shot."

"Neither do I, but there's nothing I can do about it. We're already involved. The question is, how are the gypsies involved? I recognized the man watching me, a member of Draghici's clan. We don't know nearly enough about them or Harper's associates."

Michael snorted. "Enough to what, pray tell?"

"I don't know. Expose them?"

"Harper and his friends are very serious and quite deadly, love. Getting mixed up with them would put us on the short end of things every time, I'm afraid."

"Do you think Paddington can get to the bottom of this on his own?"

"Paddington is a good policeman. If anyone can do it, he can."

"If this were a typical theft or murder, I would agree with you. But what's involved here, Michael, goes beyond anything Paddington is used to. He was practically rolling his eyes at any mention of the history involved in this affair last night. And we can't ignore the fact that he would like to shove all of this under the rug if he could. He's all but admitted to us that he's here to retire."

"I know."

"And you also know as well as I do that history is tied into the solution of this mystery."

"Yes, I do."

"We have faces, thanks to Paddington. Surely that gives us something of an edge."

Rolling over onto his side to look at her, Michael brushed an errant lock of hair from her forehead. "Not much of one. And I don't like our chances. If anything, whoever is behind this would want to kill us even more if we saw their faces. And there are probably even more members of his crew that we wouldn't know until they killed us."

"It'll be all right." Molly touched his cheek. "When did you come to bed?"

"Late."

She frowned. "You need your rest."

Michael captured her hand and kissed her fingers. "I won't rest until you're safe. And I'd feel better if you stayed home today."

"With everything going on at the marina?" Molly grimaced. "No chance of that. People will be at each other's throats and work will grind to a halt. I have a vested interest in this project. If I can help, I want to be available."

He didn't like it, but he knew she wouldn't stay away from the marina as long as she felt needed. And, truth to tell, she probably was. Molly was good at interfacing in trying situations.

He leaned toward her and kissed her. "Well, love, if I can't dissuade you, I can at least delay you."

"WELL, DON'T YOU LOOK RESTED." Iris sat at the breakfast table with Nanny.

Chagrined, Molly headed for the coffee. Michael started his mornings with tea, but she preferred coffee. The aroma filled the kitchen. "Sorry. I thought for sure you'd sleep in after the late night and the time difference."

"I've never been one for sleeping in late." Nanny had a cup of coffee and toast in front of her. "I felt guilty getting up before anyone else, except I discovered Iris is also an early riser."

"She is." Molly leaned a hip against the island and sipped her coffee.

"Would you like breakfast?"

"I can get it, Iris."

"I've already got Michael's favorite waffle batter waiting for him to come down, but I've sliced some fruit and it won't take but a moment to fix eggs and warm up the bacon I fried this morning."

"That sounds lovely."

"How do you want your eggs?"

"Over easy, please."

"Would you like to eat here or in the dining room?" Iris busied herself at the stove.

"Here would be fine." Molly slid into one of the chairs at the table. She was a bit self-conscious about Iris making her breakfast as Nanny watched. "Iris isn't exactly a housekeeper or chef."

"Is that a jab at my culinary skills, Molly?"

"No, Iris, I just…" Then Molly realized she'd been set up.

"Iris has already explained that she feels like a member of the family, not an employee." Nanny smiled.

"Too true." Michael strode into the room, carrying his notebook computer in a messenger bag. "A proper employee would know her place and not get so cheeky with the boss." He helped himself to the tea service. He sniffed. "Is that waffles I smell?"

"It is." Iris looked at him with mock insolence. "Care to strike your colors now, sir?"

"Consider them stricken. You have me in your complete thrall, Iris." Michael leaned over and gave Iris a peck on the cheek. "You know, if Mrs. Graham hadn't begged me to marry her, I'd be after making an honest woman of you."

Iris flushed slightly, but Molly knew the woman enjoyed the attention. Michael was the son that Iris had never had, and her devotion to him showed.

"You are an incorrigible flirt. And in front of your missus."

"If it's any consolation, I'll quietly eat those waffles in shame." Michael took a stool at the island and plucked a grape from a bowl. He opened the messenger bag and set up the computer.

"Where are you going today?" Molly watched him as he pulled up the browser and started jumping through websites.

"I thought I'd have a word with Inspector Paddington."

"But that's not what's occupying your ever-busy mind."

He smiled. "Remember the model of the town that I built, the one that fits together into a three-dimensional object? I realized what it is—it's a map."

"A map? Of what?"

Michael brought up pictures on the computer screen

as Nanny and Molly walked over behind him. "Charles Crowe built a miniature version of Blackpool as it was back in his day and donated the model to the local library. I got interested in the way it was built, how the odd-shaped buildings seemed to fit together. He was quite the gamesman, Charles Crowe was. After Aleister removed the model from the library, Rohan helped me construct one of my own."

"My grandson was always clever with his hands."

"More clever than I was. It was Rohan who built the models in such exact proportion. If not for his efforts, I would have never discovered that the buildings folded up into each other."

On the computer screen, Michael pulled up a representation of the three-dimensional model he and Rohan had built. Molly watched in fascination even though she'd seen the process before.

"Here the town is as Charles Crowe represented it in his model." Michael tapped keys. "Now watch this."

In response, the buildings on the three-dimensional model started folding into each other almost perfectly. When the interlocking pieces all stopped moving, a cube spun slowly on the screen.

"That, Nanny, is a fiendishly clever puzzle box. I can't even begin to imagine the time and effort Charles Crowe put into creating such a thing. The model replicates the architecture of the town, and many of the buildings were designed by Crowe himself. That just goes to show how much influence the man had over Blackpool at the time."

"One man can't build a town like that." Nanny's voice was calm and quiet. "One man, he don't have the power to do such things."

Michael's brow furrowed and he leaned back. "Charles Crowe wouldn't have wielded that much influence by himself, no. He must have had partners. Wealthy partners. People who had a considerable stake in his enterprises."

"The most profitable business Charles Crowe was involved in at the time seems to have been slave trading," Nanny suggested.

"Which was illegal. But he was willing to run the risks for money while others stood even further in the shadows and raked in their own bloody profits." Michael looked at the older woman. "You realize we're talking about a conspiracy, don't you? Several people working in collusion?"

"I'm surprised that you ever thought it could be anything less." Nanny nodded at the screen. "I've read the stories surrounding the discovery of the *Seaclipse*. There's no reason to believe that was the only ship Charles Crowe had committed to the slave trade. Then there is the murder of that man, Jeremy Chatwhistle. The captain in the West Africa squadron?"

"What do you mean?" Michael sipped his tea.

"It's plain as the nose on your face, if you ask me." Nanny shook her head. "Someone had to have informed Charles Crowe he had a West African squadron captain nipping at his heels. As Mr. Hume-Thorson's friend verified, Chatwhistle's reports were filed in London. But once Chatwhistle disappeared, the pursuit of the *Seaclipse* and its owner was dropped. Clearly somebody with a lot of influence convinced the officers of the Royal Navy their careers were better served by focusing on traders off the coast of Africa, not in their own country." Nanny nodded at the computer screen. "Now what does this puzzle box mean?"

"The way I have it figured, the exposed surfaces of the box, once it's folded, reveal the passageways and tunnels beneath Blackpool." Michael shrugged unhappily. "Some of them have changed over the past hundred and seventy years, but enough should remain to allow the passages to be identified."

"Have you been able to do that?"

"Not yet. I'm hoping I can find the connecting passages beneath the buildings if the shop owners will let me explore. Not many of them will be happy with the idea, I suspect."

"Part of their reticence is due to me, I'm afraid." Molly tapped her coffee cup. "The town is nearly divided over whether the renovations I got funding for are helpful or hurtful to Blackpool."

"And a lot of them are already tired of hearing about Charles Crowe's mythical fortune," Michael added. "It's been a local legend for over a century, and when the gold coins were found a couple of months ago, everyone got stirred up again. The furor just died down. I doubt many will wish it back."

Nanny leaned in closer. "What are these markings in the corners of the cube faces?"

Michael tapped keys again. This time as the cube slowly spun, glowing symbols were copied from the faces and dropped into a neat row at the bottom of the screen.

They included a square, a hexagon, a line, a triangle, a pentagon and a set of parallel lines.

"I don't know. I only added those recently. I noticed they were marked on the original model and I transferred them from the pictures I took of it." Michael let out a frustrated breath. "So far, I haven't been able to fathom their secret. But I believe they're part of the map. Clues to this treasure trove he reputedly left behind."

"Do you believe there is a fortune?" Nanny asked.

Michael shrugged. "I can't say. Maybe it was all spent long ago. Maybe Charles Crowe never got around to creating the nest egg he intended. There's a lot we don't know about that man."

"What about the tribal artifacts? According to my ancestor, Charles Crowe took pride in his collection and went out of his way to accumulate new pieces. And they turned up just recently, still in the possession of the Crowes."

"If they weren't worth much at the time, why would Charles Crowe acquire them and why would his descendants keep them?"

"I can't speak to the current Crowes, but my ancestor says it was because Charles Crowe believed those objects brought him a dark power, that they would help him triumph over his enemies and secure his authority." Nanny shook her head. "Others whispered that those objects carried curses for anyone that shed the blood of the people they rightfully belonged to."

A chill skated down Molly's back.

CHAPTER ELEVEN

PADDINGTON KEPT MICHAEL waiting in his office for nearly two hours. Under other circumstances, Michael might have been irritated, but he occupied himself with his computer and sifted through the news videos and YouTube podcasts that some of the more enterprising residents and media people had put together on the shooting. By the time he was told that the inspector would see him, Michael had amassed an interesting amount of material that he hadn't expected to get.

The Blackpool police department had taken up residence in an old Victorian that hadn't been updated in any way other than to add necessary electronics and knock down a few non-load-bearing walls to create more open space. The place tended to darkness and felt heavy.

Since Michael knew the way, he headed off himself. When he passed Lockwood Nightingale, the solicitor pointedly ignored him.

Paddington's office was in the rear. Photographs and awards spanning his career hung on the walls. He'd been a cop in London, then had worked his way up and plateaued. He'd planned on riding out his last few years in Blackpool in relative semiretirement.

"Come in, Mr. Graham." Paddington sorted through papers on his desk.

Michael sat in one of the two chairs in front of

the inspector's desk. "I just passed Nightingale in the hall."

"That man is annoying. Filled right to the top with flummery."

"Not a good morning?"

Paddington gestured at the small television in a corner of the room. On screen, a reporter stood in front of the Merciful Angels Hospital. "You'd think there was nothing else happening in the world."

"Perhaps it only seems that way to you."

The inspector heaved a sigh. "Mr. Graham, *perhaps* we could get to the point of this meeting. You've been waiting long enough that I thought you would have surely gotten tired of sitting out there."

"After the first couple of hours, things get easier."

"I'll try to remember that."

Michael placed his notebook computer on the desk. "May I show you something?"

"Is there any way I can stop you?"

"You'll want to see this." Michael opened up the file with the three-dimensional rendering of the library model of Blackpool.

AFTER TWO SOLID HOURS of meetings, stroking bruised egos and putting out fires, Molly was ready for a brief respite. She wasn't supposed to be so involved with the marina's remodeling, but since some of the marina fund had been stolen and members of the planning committee had been arrested a couple of weeks ago, Molly had had to step in. She walked down the harbor boardwalk, the new one, though it was new only in places, toward Grandage's Bait and Tackle for a coffee.

As she passed by Coffey's Garage, she remembered

that the young woman whose flat the sniper had used worked there. Molly struggled to recall the young woman's name, then changed direction and headed toward the garage.

Beaten and weathered tin covered the building's exterior. Salt water had finally clawed under coats of paint and eaten into the metal, leaving rusty brown age spots that had crumbled away in places. New pieces of tin had been screwed into place over some blemishes and painted as close to the original color as possible.

When the renovation of the marina had begun, Molly had tried to convince the owner, Randall Coffey, to upgrade the building, but so far the man had remained adamant. As Coffey had put it, his family's business had run that way and in that location for generations and he saw no reason to change. The place remained an eyesore, but Blackpool residents and frequent guests in town continued to take their boats and vehicles to Randall Coffey.

She found him standing under the hood of an antique American pickup. Coffey was a lean, rawboned man just short of sixty, his long gray hair pulled back in a ponytail that hung past his shoulder blades. His short-cropped beard was a little lighter gray. The sleeves of his canvas work shirt had been torn off and military tattoos of a stalking panther faded on his upper arms.

"Afternoon, Mrs. Graham." Coffey cleaned a wrench with a grease-stained red rag.

"Afternoon, Mr. Coffey. I see you're hard at work." Molly had to speak loudly to be heard over the constant whir and chatter of air-assisted power wrenches.

"I always am. Otherwise I'd have to close up shop and think about financing a retirement."

Molly smiled at that. There were Blackpool residents who insisted Randall Coffey still had the first dime he'd ever made.

"You come here snooping around after young Kate, Mrs. Graham?"

Knowing that any attempt to avoid the question would only be scoffed at, Molly fessed up. "I did."

Coffey frowned. "I figured you or the mister, or probably both, would have been by yesterday."

"Unfortunately, we were detained."

"So I heard. Bad bit of business at the hospital."

"It was."

Coffey nodded to the rear of the shop. "You'll find her in the back, tearing a boat motor apart. She hasn't been talking to the reporters that have been by. Don't know what you expect to learn. That poor child didn't see nothing nor nobody. Some miscreant just broke into her house is all. Can't stop you from wasting your time, though. Seems like some folks have got a lot of it to waste."

"Thank you, Mr. Coffey."

"Don't overstay your welcome, Mrs. Graham. This is a working garage. If the wrenches aren't turning, we're not making a profit. I make sure all my mechanics remember that."

Molly skirted the pickup and headed to the rear of the shop. Air-pressure lines and tool carts appeared to her to lie everywhere with reckless abandon, but the half-dozen men Coffey had working for him seemed to know exactly where everything was.

She found Kate laboring at a stained wooden table. A large motor lay in pieces at her feet and scattered across the table. Molly recognized the young woman from the newspaper pictures and television footage.

Only a few inches over five feet, Kate was a petite young woman dressed in a sleeveless coverall. Colorful tattoos stained her arms from wrist to shoulder, most of them of dragons and fish. Her ginger-colored hair barely touched her shoulders and frizzed in all directions. She noticed Molly's approach at once and watched her from the corner of her eye.

"Hello, Kate. I'm—"

The young woman finished tightening a bolt and looked up in disdain. "You're Mrs. Graham."

"Molly. That's right. I thought maybe I could talk to you briefly."

"Ain't got nothing to say and I don't know nothing, neither."

"I haven't asked you anything yet."

"You don't have to. Ain't but one thing people want to talk to me about these days." She turned her attention back to the motor. "Until yesterday, nobody in this town cared nothing about me, nor what I did. Didn't realize how much I liked that till it was gone."

The resentment rolled off the woman in waves. Molly remembered being that young, but she'd never been that bitter. Still, she saw the vulnerability that was there for any young woman that age.

"I'm not here to force you to talk, Kate."

"The likes of you don't intimidate me. I breathe the same air as you do, and I'm just as entitled to it."

"I'm here because my husband's friend Rohan Wallace may be in trouble. You probably know Rohan. Maybe you know Michael, as well."

At first Kate didn't reply. Then she shrugged. "I seen

'em round. We favor some of the same taverns. 'Course, here in Blackpool, it ain't as if you got a lot of places to do your drinking."

Molly didn't go to many of the bars Michael frequented when he was out on the town. "My husband's worried about Rohan. So am I."

"Breaking and entering into Crowe's Nest?" Kate shook her head. "Way I hear it, Rohan didn't have no history of that. The judge will probably go lenient on him."

"We're not concerned about the legal problems of his situation. We're more troubled by what happened at the hospital."

"You mean that man getting shot."

"I do."

"Whoever took that bloke out is long gone."

"I wish I could believe that."

Kate tapped a wrench against the motor irritably. "Why would someone like that stick around this place?"

"Maybe to shoot Rohan, too."

That caught the young woman's attention. She looked up at Molly with renewed interest. "Why do you think he's the next target?"

"Because I don't believe the sniper just chanced upon that vantage point to shoot from. I think he deliberately chose your flat. But I don't know if he was trying to kill Timothy Harper or waiting for an opportunity to kill Rohan."

"Either way, he's long gone by now. Won't be no more bother."

"I hope what you're saying is true, but I have to plan on the man still being here."

"Why?"

"Because I don't want Rohan to be hurt." Molly paused. "I don't think you want that, either."

"Ain't up to me."

"I heard you have a boyfriend."

"Sure, a regular guy. He's up in London now. Trying to find a job."

"Must be hard being away from him."

Kate gazed up at Molly suspiciously. "Sometimes. But I know he's doing it for us."

"It's still difficult getting left behind."

The young woman shrugged. "My choice. I've been to London a few times. Don't like it there. Don't like it here, either, but I hate the big cities even more. Too loud. Too busy. He'll come back once he's made some money." She returned her attention to her work.

"It must be frightening."

"What?"

"Thinking that maybe he'll decide *he* likes it there and won't come home."

"You haven't a clue what you're talking about."

"You don't think I was your age?" Molly smiled. "When I was at university, I got involved with a guy. Thought it was forever love."

She looked at Molly again. "Michael?"

"No. Not Michael."

Kate paused, then reached for a bottled soft drink she had sitting on the bench.

"His name was Caleb," Molly said. "He was a football player. He turned pro his senior year. I still had two years to go. I wanted to finish my degree, possibly get a master's, before I started chasing him all over the country. He told me that he'd be faithful." Molly shrugged. The story was true, but it had happened to one of her sorority sisters, not her. She'd made her own mistakes, but not that one. "Maybe he was. For a while. But in the end, he decided he couldn't be torn between what he loved... and me."

"But you got Mr. Graham in the end. You two seem like you get on all right."

"We do. But Mr. Graham also got me." Molly smiled and winked conspiratorially. "Our relationship isn't a one-way street. After Caleb, I thought I'd never love again. And I didn't for a very long time. Till I met Michael. Even then, it wasn't easy. Some of the same old problems were there."

"Him being British and you being American?"

Molly nodded. "One of the biggest hurdles we had to cross. And whichever way it had gone, wherever we'd ended up, I know we'd have been happy. It's just how we are. But I didn't know that at first." She looked at the young woman. "Sometimes, when you're afraid you're going to get your heart broken, it's easier to protect yourself by finding other guys who remind you that you're attractive."

Kate sipped her drink and thought about that.

"Paddington doesn't buy the way you tell it, either, Kate. Not really. He doesn't believe that sniper just happened onto your flat with its excellent view of the hospital. But he's not pushing it, because he doesn't think it's really going to matter. I don't have that luxury, because Michael keeps putting himself on the line for Rohan. That whole friendship thing. I don't want Michael's good heart to end up getting him killed."

For a moment, Molly was sure she was getting through

to Kate. Then the young woman sighed and cursed. She put the bottle down.

"I knew the guy that probably took those shots. I was the one that brought him to my flat."

CHAPTER TWELVE

KATE'S VOICE WAS SOFT and she glanced furtively around. "My boyfriend doesn't know any of this and I'd rather he didn't. Just in case he decides he's had enough of big cities one day."

"He won't hear it from me. I didn't come to cause problems, Kate."

"I met this guy in the bar. He came on to me. Funny and outgoing, he was." Kate shrugged. "I figured him for a one-night stand…you see? I was feeling blue and lonely, and I wanted company just for the night. Instead, next thing I know, this bloke has moved in. Not lock, stock and barrel, mind you. But he's staying there all the time. Kind of creeped me out, but it was also kind of cool. And this guy, he was one of the best lovers I've ever had."

"What is his name?"

"Rick. That's all he give me. Just Rick."

"Ever pick up Rick's mobile and have a look at his address book?"

"No. Thought about it, but he slept with that thing wrapped in his fist, I swear. The only time he ever put it down was when he was holding on to me." Kate colored a little at that. "Makes me sound bad, don't it?"

"No. I understand. Maybe you think so right now,

Kate, but you're going to find that you're not so very different from a lot of women your age."

"Maybe." Kate shrugged. Her eyes looked misty. "I heard about the shooting on the news. I was here. Working on this rubbish."

"Have you seen Rick since yesterday?"

Kate shook her head. "Once the police let me back into my flat, it was like he'd never even been there. All his stuff, what there was of it, was gone. He traveled light. Everything he had fit in one bag."

And you didn't connect him to the shooting? Molly wanted to ask that but didn't. "Did you have a number where you can reach him?"

"No. Wasn't no sense in it. The only place I ever seen him after I met him in the pub was my flat. Coffey don't like personal phone calls here on the job. Surprised he let you back here."

"Is there anything else you can tell me about Rick?"

"No." Kate's shoulders slumped in defeat. "I knew he was a wrong one, Molly, but I didn't let it stop me. I should've."

"Kate, all of us have things in our pasts that we'd rather not admit to. It doesn't do any good to dwell on them. So my advice to you is, don't."

"What should I tell my boyfriend?"

"You'll know when the time comes. I promise." Molly shot a glance at Coffey. "I should probably go and let you get back to your day. I've taken up enough of your time."

"Sure."

"But I appreciate you telling me this."

"Don't see that it helped."

"It did. It proves that Rick had a plan. He wasn't just a guy who happened on a good place to shoot from."

"You think he was watching over Rohan? Waiting to shoot him?"

"Maybe. Or maybe he was waiting for Timothy Harper."

"Either way, he was trouble and plenty of it."

For a moment, Molly considered how things might have gone if Kate had been seen talking to the police.

"Got something for you. Be right back." Kate walked to a bank of dented olive-green lockers, twirled the combination dial on one of them and reached inside. She took out a mobile. "Rick never let me get close to his mobile, but I had mine. Took some snaps of him while he was sleeping. Gimme your number and I'll text them to you."

Molly did, then watched as six pictures of a tall, dark-complexioned man with longish hair fed into her mobile. The man was ruggedly good-looking, and he didn't appear much older than Kate. Molly could easily see why the younger woman had gone for the guy.

She also thought he looked familiar. She took just a moment to forward the pictures to Michael's mobile, then thanked Kate again and left the garage.

"Be careful out there, Mrs. Graham." Coffey waved to her.

She wondered what he meant by that.

"Lot of strangers in town, is all."

"Thank you, Mr. Coffey. If you should ever decide you want to remodel the exterior of this garage, I'm sure I can get you a deal."

Coffey grinned. "This place will fall down around my ears before I remodel it. If it isn't broke, don't fix it.

My grandfather taught me that, and his taught him that before then. And all of 'em learned it right here in this garage."

OUTSIDE, MOLLY HEADED FOR Grandage's Bait and Tackle again, still intent on getting a cup of coffee from somewhere. The marina held more pedestrians than earlier, and the harbor had filled up with boats.

She took a deep breath as she surveyed the sights. Blackpool was having growing pains, ones that would only continue because the little town was going to gain more tourist trade and possibly a few more residents from the outside world. She didn't see that as a bad thing, but part of her realized she didn't want Blackpool to change too much.

A powerboat pulled up to the pier ahead of her and the bump of contact sent a shiver through the floating dock. Raucous rap music cascaded over the boardwalk and drew ire from the onlookers. If the group in the boat didn't settle down, the harbormaster would be along and fine them. Molly was surprised to note that one of the passengers was Lydia Crowe, Aleister Crowe's younger sister.

Like her brother, Lydia had aristocratic features. But instead of being dark as her older brother was, she had golden blond hair. She was more than ten years younger, too. Barely twenty.

She also had a figure that instantly switched on every male radar in the vicinity. Today she wore a two-piece bikini with mismatched colors. Her top, what there was of it, was pale green and her thong bikini bottoms were electric blue. Dark-lensed sunglasses covered her blue eyes.

Only one other girl was in the powerboat. She paled in comparison to Lydia, but she seemed content to bask in her reflection. Five young men with bronzed skin and bleached hair whooped and hollered in the powerboat, high-fiving each other and cracking open beers.

Evidently this was how the young elite handled the beach scene.

At first, Molly thought Lydia was going to walk on past her without saying a word. She was actually hoping for that. The less interaction Molly had with the Crowes at the moment, the better she liked it.

But no, Lydia stopped on a dime, hooked her sunglasses with a finger and surveyed Molly. "Mrs. Graham."

Molly smiled. "Yes, Lydia," she replied, as if speaking to a child.

"I thought that was you."

"Is there something I can help you with?" Molly asked.

"Not really. It's just that after everything that happened yesterday, I'm surprised to see you here."

"Where else would I be?"

Lydia shrugged. "Home. Safe."

"I think I'm safe enough here."

"Oh."

"You have a good day, Lydia."

For a moment, Lydia clearly didn't know how to take being dismissed so casually. Then she turned on her heel, put on a smile and pushed her sunglasses back into place.

Molly's gaze drifted to a reflection in the window of Grandage's Bait and Tackle. Only a short distance up the pier stood one of Stefan Draghici's clan. The same long-haired gypsy Molly had seen the previous day stood in the midst of a group of tourists.

Startled, Molly dropped a hand into her purse and took out her mobile. She brought up the camera screen. Focused on the man's reflection in the window, she placed his position in her mind and spun quickly, bringing the iPhone device up.

He was gone. Vanished like fog in a stiff wind.

"Mrs. Graham."

The deep, rumbling voice came from behind Molly. Paranoid and feeling exposed and vulnerable, she turned around again. The gypsy stood watching her with a mocking smile.

"Excuse me." Molly took a step back. "Do I know you?"

He smiled, but there was nothing mirthful about the expression. "No, but I thought we could make each other's acquaintance today."

"All right." Molly waited, but the man seemed content to just stand there. "I'm sorry, I didn't get your name."

"I didn't give it. Just think of me as the friendly sort, a man with the best interests of you and your husband at heart."

Although the words held no threat, Molly's warning signals went on full alert. She took a step back.

"Oh, you don't have anything to worry about with me, Mrs. Graham." The gypsy smiled. "If I'd meant you any harm, you'd never have seen me coming. For the moment, Stefan wants you left alone."

"I really don't have time to talk right now."

"Of course you don't. You and Mr. Graham being busy people and all. But that's all right. No foul here. When you see Mr. Graham, though, tell him Stefan would like to have a word with him. Maybe compare notes on this little treasure hunt the two of you are on."

"We're not on a treasure hunt."

The gypsy winked broadly. "Sure you aren't. All the same, let your husband know Stefan would like to see him sometime." He touched his head scarf and continued along the boardwalk.

Molly shivered and couldn't help feeling as if she'd just been broadsided by a tropical storm.

"WANT TO TELL ME WHAT IT IS I'm looking at, Michael?" Paddington listened to Michael's explanation about the puzzle box, but his expression spoke tomes about his boredom and low threshold of patience. Michael switched gears.

"Do you know what YouTube videos are, Inspector?" Michael selected one of his prechosen screens and launched it, quickly blowing it up to full screen.

"Music videos and homegrown film clips. Rubbish. Perhaps you've got time to spend looking at such things, but I don't."

On screen, footage of the shooting at Merciful Angels Hospital rolled. Michael muted the narrator, an excited male who was freaked out by the events.

"Not exactly home movies, is it, Inspector?"

Paddington growled unhappily.

"A number of law-enforcement departments are using YouTube videos of crime scenes to back up what's captured by their own photographers." Michael had read about that in *Wired* magazine and other digital sources. The knowledge had led him to his online scavenger hunt that morning, and he'd been surprised at the results.

"So? If I wanted to see video of the crime scene

yesterday, all I'd have to do is bring up the archived files."

"You've been over them?"

"Not yet. But I will soon."

"Then maybe you'll see this man." Michael stopped the video feed at two minutes and thirty-nine seconds. He took a screen capture, then opened a picture manager, dumped the capture into it and cropped the picture to blow up the face of one particular man he'd spotted in the crowd on the other side of the yellow crime-scene tape.

The man had the sharp, pointed features of a fox, sandy hair and freckles. Aviator glasses hid his eyes. Dressed in a Sex Pistols concert shirt and in his thirties, he looked like a tourist.

"Recognize him?"

Paddington pulled a file from the corner of his desk, opened it and flipped through a stack of mug shots. After a moment, he took one out and laid it on the desk. "Philip Wickersham."

"I recognized him from the pictures you had at dinner of the gang Timothy Harper belonged to. I'm guessing he was there to verify the kill."

Reluctantly, Paddington nodded.

"You don't have to feel like you're telling me any state secrets. I researched Harper on the internet and turned up some surprising results." Michael clicked in the folder he'd dropped to the bottom of his screen and article after article scrolled open. "Wickersham works for Leland Darrow, who is—by all accounts that I found—a dangerous man. Darrow runs a crew of thugs. The newspapers and magazine articles insist that he's the kind of man you

hire when you want something lifted or someone killed."
He paused, letting the information sink in again. "What
are this man and his people doing in Blackpool?"

CHAPTER THIRTEEN

PADDINGTON LEANED BACK in his chair, which squeaked as it shifted, and looked at Michael. "Don't you think that the real question is what was Rohan Wallace doing hanging about with such a man?"

Michael sat forward, resting his elbows on his knees. He'd already been turning that question around in his mind, and he was satisfied with the answer he'd arrived at. "Rohan didn't know he was involved with Leland Darrow."

"You can't just say that."

"I can. Do you remember what I told you about Harper's questions for Rohan in the hospital? He said he was on the run from someone who was after him. He told Rohan, 'these guys I've got chasing me.' Not 'chasing *us.*' Chasing '*me.*'"

"Circumstantial at best. Harper may have only been concerned for himself."

"I think Harper used Rohan to get into Crowe's Nest."

"Harper wouldn't have needed Rohan."

"That makes my point even more strongly. I believe Rohan was taken into the house to act as the fall guy in case they were caught. Harper had another agenda, and he got crossways with his mates and Leland Darrow. They killed him for whatever they thought he did."

"Interesting theory, but what would the likes of Leland Darrow and his crew want inside Aleister Crowe's home?"

"I've been trying to figure that out, but I haven't come up with a good answer. Whatever money Crowe keeps on the property wouldn't be enough for Darrow. They're used to playing for much higher stakes."

"The Crowes have a lot of valuable things."

"Those valuable things would need to be fenced." During the early years of his gaming career, Michael had designed a futuristic RPG game that dealt with interstellar thieves. He knew the lingo and the particulars. "If you have to fence a haul, you're taking pennies on the pound. Most professional art thieves make their money selling stolen items back to their owners or the insurance companies. According to everything I read, that's not how Darrow and his lot operate."

Paddington rubbed the back of his neck. "There are days, Mr. Graham, wonderful beer notwithstanding, that you give me a headache."

"If I'm wrong, just say so. I'll close up my computer and take my leave."

The inspector gave that option some consideration. "At this point, I can't say that you're wrong. I've been exploring the same question. But I'd wager that Rohan Wallace was used as more than just a scapegoat. I'm thinking that Harper, or maybe Darrow himself, believed Rohan Wallace could help them find whatever it was they were looking for. That Mr. Wallace indeed had some inside knowledge of the matter."

Michael wasn't happy with that response. "The treasure?"

"Everyone seems to be more interested in it than ever,

what with the discovery of that ship and the coins. Why not?"

"Because treasure hunting isn't the kind of thing that Darrow would choose to get involved with. It's too uncertain."

"People change. Crime and criminals aren't that hard to figure out. Usually the shortest line between two points will give you the perpetrator you're after. Contrary to popular fictions, all criminals are not masterminds."

"We seem to have attracted a few of those to Blackpool recently."

"But in the end, they weren't clever enough, were they?"

Michael didn't respond. In recent months, he and Molly had been responsible in a large part for the apprehension of a few of those people. Solving crimes hadn't ever been something they'd cared to do outside of mystery novels, shows, movies and games, but they'd had a good run on their "cases."

His iPhone buzzed for attention, announcing that he'd received a text. He picked it up, looked at the text and picture, then blew it up to fill the screen.

"Molly got a picture of the man that was in the flat rented by the girl who works for Coffey." Michael showed the inspector the image.

"Kate Ashcroft? Where did she get that?"

"Apparently she had more success with Kate Ashcroft than you did."

Paddington cursed softly. "I knew that little twit wasn't telling me everything. I also think she's very lucky to be alive." He squinted at the image, then shifted his attention to the mug shots. After a moment, he selected another one and pushed it onto the desk. "Salvatore Gnucci."

"Doesn't sound like a native."

"Born in Liverpool, though."

"I didn't turn him up in my searches."

"He's a recent addition to Darrow's crew. And you won't find everything on YouTube. This one specializes in sniping."

"He was at Kate's flat for several days."

Paddington thought about that. "Plenty of time for him to have killed Rohan Wallace if that was the objective. They were watching over Rohan, waiting to see if he came round. When Harper showed up and looked like he was going to get caught by you, they decided to eliminate loose ends."

"They could have killed Harper before he got inside the hospital."

"Perhaps they *wanted* him to talk to Mr. Wallace."

Feeling excited because he thought they were on to something, Michael nodded. "Harper was the only one of them that Rohan had met. Maybe they felt Rohan would have trusted Harper."

"It was still foolishness. The man was in a coma. Mr. Wallace wasn't talking to anyone."

"They might not have believed that." Michael paused. "At any rate, I think that gives more support to your theory that Darrow and company were using Rohan to get inside Crowe's Nest."

"That's not my theory, Mr. Graham." Paddington tapped a blunt finger on the desk. "But…it definitely is a theory."

Although he didn't exactly feel at peace about the turn of events, Michael couldn't help smiling in triumph.

Then his mobile buzzed again. The message this time wasn't so rewarding.

MOLLY SIPPED HER COFFEE, then dropped the paper cup into a nearby bin when she spotted Michael striding down the boardwalk. Paddington and Krebs were hot on his heels.

Michael was focused entirely on her. She loved it when he gave her that kind of attention, but she didn't care for the circumstances.

"Hello, love." He smiled at her, but he glanced around warily. Anger burned in his sapphire-blue eyes.

"Now that you're here, I feel foolish about calling you."

"With everything going on, I'm glad you did." Michael took off his black leather jacket and draped it across her shoulders. "Have you seen this man since he introduced himself?"

Molly shook her head.

Paddington talked briefly on his mobile, then folded it and put it away. "Owen Montcalm knows where we can find Stefan Draghici, Mrs. Graham. Do you feel up to having a word with him? Maybe it's time we pushed back."

"I'd be happy to, Inspector."

OWEN MONTCALM, BLACKPOOL'S harbormaster, occupied a small building not far from Grandage's Bait and Tackle. Bald and wearing oil-stained overalls, Montcalm stood outside the building with a clipboard.

"Afternoon, Inspector, Sergeant Krebs, Mr. and Mrs. Graham." Montcalm touched his hat.

"Owen." The inspector stopped in front of the man.

"I've been searching through records as you asked, Inspector, and I believe I've found Draghici's boat." Montcalm flipped over a page and revealed a photocopied color picture of a marine operator's license. The face on the license wasn't one Molly recognized.

Michael looked impressed. "I didn't know you were investigating Draghici, Inspector."

Paddington shrugged. "Nothing official, but under the circumstances, with Draghici getting underfoot at every opportunity lately, I thought I'd dig a little deeper into his business. He comes and goes from Blackpool a lot. Since I don't believe for a minute that he just vanishes, I figured he had to have a boat. I asked Owen to check through the records."

"The boat's registered to Amos Decarran." The harbormaster spelled the last name.

Paddington looked back at Krebs, but the unflappable sergeant was already on her mobile and talking to someone.

"What do you know about Decarran?" Paddington flipped through the papers himself.

Montcalm shook his head. "Not much more than you see there. Lists his home port as London and sails an eighty-foot yacht."

"Doesn't sound like a typical Romany name."

Michael smiled. "Perhaps it's an alias. Or the real name of one of Draghici's people."

"Says here he's self-employed. Any guesses what Mr. Decarran does?"

"No," the harbormaster said. "I didn't talk to him much more than to get his information, his intentions and his money. Reading minds isn't part of my job description. They come in here if they have a boat and they pay me. That's the way the system works."

Paddington frowned. "Where can I find this boat, Owen?"

Montcalm pointed out into the harbor. "Yonder's the yacht. She's called *Thames Drifter.*"

"Can I borrow a boat, Owen?"

MICHAEL STEERED THE BORROWED boat because he had more skill behind the wheel than either Paddington or Krebs.

Inspector Paddington talked on his mobile, and Michael was able to get the gist of the conversation. Evidently Amos Decarran was known to the police, and his reputation with them wasn't a good one, but he wasn't wanted anywhere currently. He sounded like the kind of man that would take up with Stefan Draghici. The inspector dropped his mobile back into his pocket. "We'll want to go slow and easy with this one, Krebs."

"Yes, sir."

"Molly, Michael, I want you to be careful what you say to this man. I've got a couple more men coming over this way, but Decarran's the sort used to violence."

"That's as plain as the nose on your face." Molly stared at the yacht as Michael cut the engines to half speed.

The men aboard the *Thames Drifter* had already spotted the approaching boat and had spread out to seize tactical advantage. Michael felt nervous about the coming encounter, but he was too angry to simply walk away.

"Decarran's done some time for receivership. Was mixed up in selling boats and marine supplies with forged documents. That's the easy stuff." Paddington's eyes narrowed. "He's also suspected of piracy and murder, but none of those charges have stuck yet. Twice, the complainants disappeared just as the case was coming to court. By all accounts, he's not a man you want to be dealing with."

"Draghici sought me out, Inspector." Molly's voice was hard and flat. "If Decarran is mixed up with Draghici, Michael and I are already dealing with him."

Paddington nodded grimly. "I suppose you are at that. Well, we'll call on him today and let him know you're not alone."

"Thank you, Inspector."

"It's my pleasure. I want people in my town to walk about without worrying that the Amos Decarrans or Stefan Draghicis of the world will hurt them. We'll get this sorted."

For the first time, Michael realized that Paddington was going out of his way to help them.

As he brought the boat around with expert skill, the men aboard the yacht peered down with disdain.

"Ahoy, the boat." Paddington stood on the starboard side, in plain view.

"I hear you. State your business." A lean, hard-faced man with tattoos sleeving his arms stood at the rail. His long hair blew in the wind to reveal gold hoops dangling from his ears.

"I'm Detective Chief Inspector Paddington of the Blackpool Police. I'd like to have a word."

"We haven't done anything wrong." The man grinned and looked straight at Molly as though undressing her.

Michael had to restrain himself.

"I didn't say that you had, did I? I'm exercising my right to come aboard and look around."

"That's more the job of the coasties, isn't it?"

"Not when you're in this harbor. When you're here, you're under my purview."

"We're not entertaining at the moment, Inspector. Perhaps another time."

"No, it'll be now or I'll have this boat locked down till we get this sorted. You tell Amos Decarran and Stefan Draghici that."

"Consider him told." The loud voice floated over the boat's side just before Draghici walked into view. He was resplendent in his brightly colored garb. His black hair trailed over his shoulders. "Inspector Paddington. I would say it's nice to speak with you again, but I gather that it isn't."

"That's a fair assumption."

Draghici swept his gaze over Michael and Molly. "You've brought company."

"Thought it would be good, seeing as how you wanted to speak to Mr. Graham."

"So I did. Come aboard." Draghici gestured, and one of his crew rolled out a rope ladder. "Toss out your mooring ropes. We'll bring you alongside. Don't want anyone dropping into the water."

Michael tossed the bowline to one of the men. Paddington threw the stern line to another. They pulled the lines in close enough for the hulls to bump, then wrapped the ropes around the mooring cleats.

Paddington went up the ladder first, followed by Krebs and Molly. Michael brought up the rear and wondered what they'd gotten themselves in for.

CHAPTER FOURTEEN

BY THE TIME MOLLY REACHED the yacht's deck, Draghici had retreated to the salon. Paddington glared at the man's back as he followed him down.

"We can talk out here, Mr. Draghici."

"I prefer to chat here, Inspector. And since I'm agreeing to this meeting out of the goodness of my heart, we'll do it my way, if you please. It's far too hot and uncomfortable to stand around in the sun. And if you're going to address me, I prefer to be addressed as Captain Draghici."

Of course you do. It took real effort for Molly to keep her face neutral.

With obvious reluctance, Paddington followed the man into the salon.

"Can I get you a drink, Inspector?"

"I'm on the job here."

"Sounds serious."

"Maybe it is."

Draghici finished pouring himself a drink at the small, well-appointed wet bar that fronted the galley area. Light glinted from the rings adorning his fingers. He glanced up at Molly. "Would you like a drink, dear lady?"

The way he said the words sounded offensive. "No, thank you," Molly replied politely.

"What about you, Mr. Graham?"

"There's nothing you could offer me, mate." Michael stood, bunched like a hard knot, arms folded, his stance broad. His words sounded calm but chiseled.

Krebs turned down the offer of a drink, as well.

"Well, then, it appears I'll be drinking alone. It's a good thing I have no problem doing that." Draghici took his glass and sat at the U-shaped sofa that filled the heart of the salon.

"One of your men approached Mrs. Graham a short time ago." Paddington stood with his hands in his pockets. "I thought maybe we could talk about that."

Draghici lifted a mocking eyebrow. "A chance encounter on the street? That's enough to bring you all the way out here?" He shook his head in disbelief. "Things must surely be slow in this little town, Inspector Paddington, if the police department feels compelled to follow up on that."

"I don't put up with people under my protection being threatened."

Swiveling his attention to Molly, Draghici looked surprised, but the effort was pure ersatz. "I'm sorry, Mrs. Graham. Did one of my people in some way cause you alarm?"

Michael fielded the question and took a step forward, setting two of Draghici's goons into motion. "Your man told Molly you wanted to talk to me, mate. Here I am. So talk."

In that moment, Molly could see the young street tough Michael had been in his earlier years. He'd scuffled and fought in the pubs and neighborhoods back in London, and he'd hung with some questionable people when he was younger. But his love of video games had focused him and kept him from getting lost. Even now, his pursuits of soccer and rugby, hiking and biking attended to his love of being physical.

"You are a direct one." Draghici sipped his drink.

"Trust me, I can be more direct."

Paddington shifted slightly, taking one step to place himself between Michael and Draghici at an oblique angle. Evidently the other gypsies had read a threat in Michael's words, as well, because they moved in closer.

Draghici held a ringed hand up and his men pulled back. Then the man laughed. "All right. I wanted to speak with you about your ongoing treasure hunt here in Blackpool."

"I'm not involved in a treasure hunt, mate."

"That's not how I hear it. People tell me you've stepped up your pursuit."

"What people?" Paddington's voice filled the salon.

Draghici shrugged. "Just acquaintances that I've met since I've been here in Blackpool." He sipped his drink again. "They say that you've been looking for Charles Crowe's treasure."

"I don't believe such a treasure exists."

"Then why are you snooping around?"

"I like looking at unusual things. Do you know anything about me?"

"I know that you're a rich man."

"Any idea how I got that way?"

"I heard something about games or some such."

"Video games," Michael said. "Computer games. Things with involved histories and physical research. That's what I'm doing. Research."

"Seems like an awful lot of poking around just to find out information for a video game."

"I'm a craftsman. That's why I'm successful." Michael stared at Draghici. "In the future, you might want to get in touch with me before you go chasing after my wife."

"I wasn't chasing after your wife. My friend merely encountered her and thought he'd pass a message on to you. You see, I think you will want to talk to me."

Michael didn't say anything.

"My father, and his father before him, have searched for the gold Charles Crowe stole from my ancestors. My predecessors were determined to find that gold, to get it back, always hearing one story or another. And they weren't successful at what they did. They got just enough of a taste of the truth to keep them interested. Let me show you something."

Draghici got up and walked to one of the bulkhead walls, reached up and pulled down a map. The map showed the town and harbor of Blackpool, but all through it and across it, dotted lines ran willy-nilly. Upon closer inspection, Molly saw that the lines were numbered and in different colors.

"My father and grandfather have explored Blackpool before, Mr. Graham. Many times over the years." Draghici shook his head. "I've even been through many of the tunnels and passageways in and around town. Never saw anything promising enough to get my hopes up. Until those gold coins were found and I watched you become so enthusiastic in your own endeavors. That's what convinced me that we had a chance of reclaiming the riches that belong to my family.

"Then I found out about that slave ship sunk in the

harbor. The *Seaclipse*." Draghici pointed through one of the windows where Algernon and his archaeology students toiled to discover all they could about the sunken ship. "Just like that, the old certainty returned to me and I was that small boy sitting at my grandfather's knee, listening to all those stories about the magnificent treasure Charles Crowe had stolen away. I couldn't sit idly and wait."

Molly couldn't imagine Draghici waiting idly for anything. The man was too abrasive, too pushy.

"I admired how you uncovered the real murderer of the drug dealer Willie Myners and solved the business with the stolen renovation money. I thought to myself, now there's a man who knows what's what. I decided I wanted to ask you here and compare notes. Maybe we can find the treasure when no one before us has ever been able to."

Michael pursed his lips. "I'm not interested in comparing notes with you. Not now, not ever. Is that clear?"

The smile on Draghici's face was hard and fixed. He didn't like being shown up in front of his men. "Crystal."

Paddington straightened. "Now that we've got that little matter attended to, maybe you should consider dropping anchor somewhere else."

"You can't kick me out of town, Inspector."

"No, you're right about that, but I'll not have you troubling Mrs. or Mr. Graham again, or I'll lock you up for harassment. That's a promise."

Draghici waved a dismissive hand. "I believe we've exhausted this conversation."

"Indeed." Paddington turned and walked toward Michael.

Reluctantly, Michael gave ground in front of Paddington. Molly reached out and took her husband's hand, pulling him into motion.

"But I would leave you with one thought." Draghici looked smug, but Michael detected a glint of malevolent menace in the gypsy leader's eyes. "People have been known to go missing from this town. You might want to be careful in the future, since you're not welcoming my protection."

Michael started to go back for Draghici, but Paddington put a big hand in the center of his chest and restrained him. At the same instant, two of the gypsies closed ranks protectively around Draghici.

"Leave it, Michael." Paddington set off again, and this time Michael went with him.

"DID YOU BUY HIS STORY?" Michael steered the boat away from *Thames Drifter,* then opened up the throttle. He was glad to be putting distance between him and Draghici. Anger still throbbed within him and made him shake slightly. He definitely felt threatened by the gypsy leader's "cautionary" words. Molly stood at his side with her arm wrapped around his.

Paddington shrugged. "This bloody treasure has all the kooks coming out of the woodwork. Just the thought of it appears enough to drive normal people daft." The inspector glanced at Michael. "And you. I wouldn't be so high-and-mighty about others. You seem to be quite actively searching for this treasure, as well."

"I'm more interested in finding out why Leland Darrow and his people set up Rohan at Crowe's Nest.

Like I said, those people aren't here hunting treasure. You won't convince me of that."

"I'm not happy with that answer, either, Mr. Graham, but I don't know what else is afoot."

"Neither do I. Yet."

Paddington sighed. "You know, you might let this be a lesson for you."

"Draghici?"

"Yes."

Michael shook his head. "I'm not going to let the likes of him scare me." Molly squeezed his arm and he knew she was cautioning him.

"I didn't say you had to be scared, Mr. Graham, but perhaps a little extra vigilance would be in order. Draghici believes he's never been closer to that gold he claims Charles Crowe stole from his family. He's not going to continue to be careful about what he does."

Michael focused on steering the boat and didn't reply, but he seethed inside. He didn't like seeing Molly afraid, and Stefan Draghici had certainly given her pause.

LATER THAT EVENING, after dinner and while Molly was busy on the phone talking to people at the marina, Michael went up to his office to think. There, surrounded by comic books, action figures, posters of older video games, including some he'd designed, he did his best thinking.

Whole worlds unfolded in his mind when he was on a roll, and they were peopled with amazing characters, wonderful monsters, eerie landscapes and ancient settings fraught with danger and exotic puzzles.

He envied his story people their lives. They didn't really have to worry about their loved ones, and their trials and tribulations were over after a few days of intense playing.

Video games weren't like real life. In a game, he could pause the play, power the system down and walk away whenever he wanted to.

He tried to focus on the electronic copy he'd made of Nanny Myrie's journal. He'd also begun a topographical map of Blackpool and the surrounding area, plucking recognizable landmarks from the narrative and inputting them into the map he'd uploaded onto his computer. Then he mixed in all the points he'd found on the map he'd made from his model of the town. He felt certain he had a lot of spots correctly fixed, but he still didn't have a complete chronological or geographical picture of the slave trade Charles Crowe had conducted.

He was frustrated because he didn't know what to do next. Rohan was still in the hospital. Molly was still buried in the work at the marina. And he had no idea what Leland Darrow was doing in Blackpool. Stefan Draghici was another wild card.

In an attempt to alleviate stress and work through his mood, Michael opened up his email. New sketches from Keith had arrived. He opened the attachments and found the redesigns of the underwater city were absolutely amazing. That made Michael happy. He'd known Keith would come through. There was never any doubt about it.

Hey, Michael.
Hope you like the new art. If you do, I can get to work on finishing the designs straightaway so the modelers can scan them in and have their wicked way with them.

I like the new version. All it took was us getting on
the same page.
All best,
Keith

Michael fired back a quick response.

Hey, Keith.
They're bloody brill, mate. I knew you could do
it. Sorry for not making this clear the first time
through.
Yours,
Michael

As he hit the send button on his mail client, Michael
thought about what Keith had said about getting on the
same page. An idea blossomed in his mind.

He went downstairs and found Nanny and Iris engaged in a game of gin.

"Nanny, would it be possible for me to go over the
journal you brought with you?"

Nanny and Iris both glanced at him suspiciously.
"What do you plan on doing with that journal, Michael?"

"Drop a nuclear bomb into Blackpool's past and see
what floats to the top."

CHAPTER FIFTEEN

Hello, Aleister

I've recently come across new documents that reveal more of what Charles Crowe was doing all those years ago. I'm thinking of maybe sending them to various media outlets and letting them run with it. Not only your family, but the families of others will have their despicable histories revealed. What do you think? Should we talk?
Sincerely,
Michael Graham

MOLLY GLANCED UP FROM the email missive on her iPhone to her husband, who looked totally worn-out and barely awake at 7:48 the next day. He closed his eyes. She grabbed his shoulder and shook him.

"Tell me you did not send this email."

"Sorry, love. I did." Michael yawned.

"Do you realize what you've done? You're waving a red flag at Aleister."

"You're not going to let me sleep, are you?"

"Not till we talk about this."

Michael rolled over onto his back and looked at her. "Okay. Talk. I'll listen."

"You shouldn't have done this."

"Too late."

"I thought we were going to discuss everything when it came to Aleister."

"Would you have let me do this if I'd told you?"

"Of course not."

"There you are. Easier to ask forgiveness than permission."

Molly shook her head. "Why? Since the *Seaclipse* has been found, it's only a matter of time before Charles Crowe's involvement in the slave trade comes to light."

"And Aleister will quickly discover that, no matter how hard he runs, he can't escape the past." Michael smiled. "It's a pretty harsh lesson, if you ask me, but I want him to pay for what he did to Rohan."

"What possible good do you imagine will come of this?"

Rolling over onto his side, Michael stared at her. Fatigue showed in his blue eyes, and so did the worry. He reached up and brushed back a lock of hair from her face. "One way or the other, love, we need answers about what's going on here."

"This issue isn't ours to deal with, Michael."

"Yet here we are, aren't we? Stuck right in the middle of everything." Michael shook his head. "After Draghici's man came to you yesterday, I decided I can't do this anymore."

"Do what?"

"Let this mystery run us. Run our lives. It's time we take our place back in the driver's seat. Paddington's just going to have to slide over a bit."

"Do you really think Aleister will reveal anything?"

"I won't know till I try." He smiled up at her. "Are you through talking?"

"No. I just don't know what else to say."

"Well, while you're thinking..." Michael reached up and captured her, pulling her back to the bed and kissing her soundly.

DESPITE MOLLY'S CONCERNS, two days passed and nothing happened. Finally, Michael got tired of waiting for the other shoe to drop and he sent his information on Crowe to Fred Purnell, the local newsman.

The phone in the bedroom rang as Michael finished tying his tennis shoes. He'd dressed in jeans and a yellow-and-black-striped London Wasps rugby jersey, expecting to have a casual day while waiting for a response from Fred. He still felt bushed, but he wasn't able to sleep any more. Molly was still in the shower.

"Hello?"

"Michael, Fred Purnell is here and would like to have a word with you." Iris sounded disapproving. "He's unannounced. At the very least, he should have called. Some people have no sense of proper manners."

Fred Purnell was the owner/editor/publisher of the *Blackpool Journal,* the weekly paper that serviced the community.

"I suppose he's standing right there, getting an earful of this?" Michael grinned. Iris Dunstead was a protective and thorough gatekeeper.

"He is."

"Then I hope he looks properly shamefaced."

"He doesn't. Not nearly enough."

"Well, his presence here isn't a surprise. I should have told you to expect him, except when I emailed him it was late. This is my fault, and I do apologize."

"No need. I'll show him to the dining room."

FRED PURNELL WAS IN HIS LATE fifties, a robust, broad-bodied man, who favored suspenders over a belt and wore his thinning hair plastered against his scalp. His salt-and-pepper beard was cut short and he wore glasses.

Iris had indeed set Purnell up in the dining room and given him a cup of tea. He sat at the table with a small notebook, writing industriously. Purnell was always working on one story or another.

"Good morning, Fred."

The publisher cocked an eyebrow. "You look like the cat that ate the canary." He flipped from the page he was on to another.

"Really? Is it a good look on me?"

"I should take a snapshot and run it on the obituary column, which will probably follow along any day now. This will stir up quite the hornet's nest."

"Will it?" Michael poured himself a cup of tea and sat.

"Most definitely."

"And is there ever any *right* way to do this?"

"Someone that can't fight back would be a better target. Someone that can't touch you would be best."

"But where would be the fun in that?"

Purnell narrowed his eyes. "All joviality aside, Michael, I'm afraid even if you haven't heard from Aleister that you've riled him up a lot."

Iris entered the dining room, carrying a tray stacked high with waffles, sausages, hash browns and fresh fruit. She handed Michael a plate, then gave one to Purnell and kept one for herself. She seated herself without being invited.

"Where did you get your information, Michael?" Purnell asked.

Michael shook his head. "I'm not telling."

"My readers are going to be curious."

"I think they're going to be more curious about the Crowe family's involvement in the illicit slave trade, not to mention their accomplices."

"We could be sued, you know."

"I don't think so. We're making no accusations." Michael gestured to the stack of waffles and Iris dug in, followed by Purnell.

"You're still slicing things mighty thin. So why do you want to publish this information?"

After a moment, Michael spoke more seriously. "Because it's time to take some of the heat off Rohan Wallace. I want people to realize that it could have been anyone among them that went to Crowe's Nest that night." He paused. "Plus, I don't know if we're going to get any answers about what happened all those years ago any other way. Too many people want to cover this up." He thought about Stefan Draghici. "And too many people want to find that bloody treasure. So either it's discovered or people learn that it's all a big story. That's what I'm after. Whichever result, Blackpool needs peace." He poured syrup over his waffles. "Molly and I need peace."

"All right. Let's talk about an exposé, then…."

"YOU REALIZE YOU'VE CREATED a PR nightmare for me, don't you?" Molly sat across the table from Michael at Peggy's Pies and Bakery the next day, where they'd agreed to meet for lunch.

The pie-and-pastry shop was crowded even at two in the afternoon. With all the new people in town, lunchtime had been extended. The restaurants and pubs did well for it, though.

"Oh, yeah." Michael rolled his eyes ruefully. "My mobile has been blowing up ever since the *Journal* piece ran. Don't know how these people got my bloody number."

Molly's heart went out to Michael when she saw the dogged tiredness clinging to him. He'd gone for the throat when Draghici had come at her. She should have known he would react in some way, but she'd been busy putting out fires at the marina renovation.

Peggy Hartwick, the strawberry blonde owner of the eatery, brought plates of steaming shepherd's pie to their table. "Be careful, loves. These are fresh and piping hot. What with all the new people in town, we have a hard time keeping up with the demand these days."

"Thank you." Michael picked up his napkin and spread it over his lap.

Molly used her fork to break open the shepherd's pie. Chopped beef, gravy, carrots, peas, onions and mashed potatoes spilled across her plate.

"Mmm… A good pie makes everything better," Michael said.

It was nice to see Michael smiling and carefree again, even if Molly knew it was going to be short-lived.

Michael took his mobile from his pocket and glanced at it. Then he smiled the way he did after he'd been stuck on a particularly involved piece of a game design and had figured out the perfect way to solve the problem. He tapped a text reply and put the mobile away. "Sorry, love. That was the call I was waiting for."

"Aleister Crowe?"

Michael smiled. "You know me far too well."

"Do you want company?"

"I don't think so."

"If I'm with you, Aleister might play nice."

"I don't want him playing nice. I want him yelling and throwing things at the walls. There's a better chance of learning things if he's out of control."

CHAPTER SIXTEEN

AT 3:28 P.M., MICHAEL CLIMBED out of his Land Rover in front of the offices Aleister Crowe kept on Bell Street. He locked the vehicle and headed for the two-story stone building that had been a pub up until nearly fifty years ago, at which time the Crowe family purchased and renovated it.

Before Michael reached the building's entrance, Crowe's dark green Jaguar XFR slid to a smooth stop at the curb. The window dropped just enough to reveal Crowe's face. "We'll talk in the car."

For a split second, Michael didn't know if he was comfortable being alone with Crowe. It wasn't that long ago that he'd seen Crowe kill a man as easily as opening a bag of crisps, and with about as much emotion. They'd been pursued by men trying to kill them because of Michael and Molly's investigation into a train robbery, but still...

Crowe impatiently tapped his black-leather-clad fingers on the steering wheel. "I don't have all day, Mr. Graham." He never even turned to face Michael.

Without a word, Michael opened the passenger door and sat in the seat adjacent to Crowe. Lockwood Nightingale was sitting in the back and didn't look happy.

"Buckle up, Mr. Graham." By the time he gave the

warning, Crowe was already under way. He drove too fast through Blackpool's twisty, winding streets.

"Where are we going?" Michael secured his seat belt but still didn't feel safe.

Crowe said nothing as he shifted smoothly, taking the corners with Grand Prix skill. The Jaguar performed like an Olympic athlete.

Pedestrians flashed by outside Michael's window, but Crowe didn't get too close to any of them. It helped that the walkers and bicyclists got out of the way when the Jaguar roared in their direction.

"You wanted to talk to me." Crowe took the final turn and powered out of Blackpool. The marina stretched along the coast to their right, but that swiftly vanished, as well.

"The mystery of Charles Crowe's treasure, whether fact or fiction, has gotten too large for Blackpool." Michael shifted slightly in the seat so he could keep an eye on both Crowe and Nightingale.

"It's a story. Nothing more. The tale never got out of hand till you and your wife started mucking about."

"I disagree. The *Seaclipse* lay out in the harbor, awaiting discovery. It was simply a matter of time before someone found it."

"What does that have to do with anything?"

"Because no one knew that Charles Crowe's fortune was gained from the illegal sale of slaves until the ship was uncovered. So was that just another secret of the aloof Crowe family? You people felt justified hiding what Charles Crowe did."

"Watch yourself, Michael." Crowe's voice was razor-sharp with warning. "Tread lightly when you're talking about my family."

Nightingale spoke up from the backseat. "Where did you get your information, Mr. Graham?"

"Is that important?"

"It is if your so-called 'evidence' was stolen from Mr. Crowe's home. It could be considered personal property."

Michael looked over the seat at the solicitor. "That's not the issue here."

"I disagree. If your source was Rohan Wallace, then it is definitely the issue, as—given his history—he likely stole it from Mr. Crowe's home. We'll start with charges of an invasion of privacy, trespassing and build from there."

"Lockwood." Crowe spoke quietly, his tone flat and cold.

Nightingale looked supremely irritated. "Aleister, I can't begin to tell you how important this is. You've seen how many phone calls I've fielded since that article appeared. It's only going to get worse as more media outlets pick it up."

"I didn't ask you to answer those calls."

"Ignoring them isn't going to make them go away. These people—very important people—are going to blame you if this story goes national. God forbid, international."

"It's probably already too late for that," Michael said.

"Do you see what I'm talking about, Aleister? This is exactly the kind of problem I've been warning you against."

"So far the story's only appeared in the *Blackpool Journal,* even with the internet. How did these 'other people' find out about the email I sent him?" Michael asked.

Crowe waved a dismissive hand. "People I do business with or against routinely spy on me. They look for dirt they can use against me. You're very naive if you didn't realize that might happen when you sent me an unencrypted email."

Michael thought maybe he had been naive. Aleister Crowe was a player in the financial fields. Or perhaps he'd subconsciously wanted Aleister Crowe to get caught out.

Nightingale glared at Michael. "These are people that care about their reputations. They're the kind that will squash you like a bug."

"This isn't just about reputations, and doing anything to me isn't going to help them now." Michael switched his attention back to Crowe and ignored the solicitor.

Crowe drove smoothly, eyes on the road. "True enough. So what do you want to talk about?"

"Have you heard of a man named Leland Darrow?"

"I read the papers." Crowe smiled thinly. "Some say that he's a criminal mastermind. Villainy for hire."

"He's involved in this now."

Crowe glanced at Michael, then looked back at the road. "What do you mean?"

Michael was sure that Paddington wouldn't be happy with him telling Crowe what he knew of the situation. The inspector had been playing the matter close to his vest. But in for a penny… "The man that was gunned down in front of Merciful Angels worked for Darrow."

"You're certain about this?"

"Quite. I helped Paddington dot the i's and cross the t's on that particular bit of information."

"Getting to be a regular detective, aren't you?" The sarcasm was as swift and biting as a wasp sting.

"Not even. The man at Merciful Angels was probably inside Crowe's Nest with Rohan Wallace that night."

"I didn't see anyone else there."

"The dead bloke—Timothy Harper—isn't the kind of man you'd see while he was on the job."

"Please." Nightingale was practically frothing at the mouth in the rear seat. "Do *not* get sucked into this, Aleister. I'm begging you. There's a lot of damage control we still have to do. We have to deny everything Graham has said. We have to ferret out his sources and condemn them for the shams they are."

"They're not shams," Michael objected.

"Oh, really? Do you have a document from that time that ties all these speculations into one neat bundle?"

"I'm not prepared to discuss that today."

"You're going to have to do it soon."

Crowe interrupted. "Tell me about Leland Darrow."

"What do you want to know?"

"Why would he be interested in me?"

"Your ancestor's treasure. Same as a lot of people."

Crowe shook his head. "Darrow is a player, from all accounts. He would only be involved for a sure payday. Despite the animosity between us, Michael, believe me when I say that whatever Charles Crowe had was long ago spent or lost forever. It just doesn't make any sense that Darrow would be interested."

Michael believed Crowe. He'd said the same thing when he'd talked to Paddington about Darrow. "Then, if Darrow is involved, there has to be another reason. Since he had a man inside Crowe's Nest, the answer must lie there."

"Or, at least, Darrow believes it does." Crowe tapped his fingers on the steering wheel.

"Aleister, come on. Please don't tell me you're buying into this tommyrot." Nightingale stared daggers at Michael. "It's just a fancy. A story he's made up to throw you off balance."

"I didn't make up the dead man at Merciful Angels, and I didn't make up the criminal record he has that ties him to Darrow." Michael focused on Crowe. "I wanted you to know about Darrow. In case there was a problem."

Nightingale cursed. "So now you want to make Aleister paranoid about some mythical criminal bogeyman? Preposterous."

"I did all of this for a reason." Michael spoke plainly. "I didn't do it specifically to harm you."

"You knew Aleister would get caught in the fallout."

"Yes. I have been, too. But we were already there. It's been like watching an accident take place in slow motion. With this much attention on Charles Crowe and that treasure, maybe the truth of the matter will set us all free."

"What truth?" Nightingale leaned forward in the seat. "What truth is that exactly, Mr. Graham? That Charles Crowe was a slave trader and a cutthroat? That hasn't been proven. Try saying that in a court of law and I'll tear you to shreds. Truth doesn't matter nearly so much as evidence."

Crowe flicked his black eyes to the rearview mirror. "Lockwood, have a care if you value your friendship with me."

"I meant no disrespect, Aleister, but what this man

is saying is balderdash. This is a smear campaign. Graham's starting with you, but he's going after bigger game. He's going to grab headlines for himself and make himself out to be some sort of hero, while you and your family's friends take a beating in the public eye."

Michael ignored him. "Think about Darrow. He's the one you should be concerned about. And there's Stefan Draghici. He approached Molly and me a couple days ago."

Crowe smiled faintly. "What did that oaf want with you?"

"To become partners in the search for your ancestor's treasure."

"Draghici's quite fanciful, isn't he?"

Michael thought about Draghici. "He is, but that doesn't make him any less dangerous. He's getting desperate."

THEY HAD MOLLY BOXED BEFORE she saw them.

She was using the keypad to unlock her car doors, still talking on the phone to one of the remodeling agents, then the men were on her.

One of them stripped her phone from her while the other screwed a metallic object against the base of her skull.

"What you feel there, Mrs. Graham, is a mighty big pistol. I pull this trigger, your head's gonna empty in a rush. If you scream or struggle, I'm going to pull the trigger. You hear me?"

"Yes." Molly forced herself to keep breathing and stay calm. All around her, the marina was in full motion. Pedestrians were everywhere, and none of them were looking at her. No one saw.

"I don't need you to talk. Just nod your head. Do you understand?"

Molly nodded.

"Walk with me and my mate back toward the street."

Feeling her knees weaken, Molly forced herself to move. She couldn't believe this was happening.

A cargo van with blank metal sides trundled along the street and stopped in front of her. When the side door rasped open, sliding along worn tracks, Stefan Draghici appeared, sitting on a small metal chair. He smiled when he saw her.

"Hello, Mrs. Graham."

Molly didn't speak.

Draghici gestured, and the two men beside Molly forced her into the van.

"It's a shame it's come to this, but I tried to be civil with your husband. He got all high-and-mighty with me." Draghici sighed as if the weight of the world was on his shoulders. "Then there was this news today. Got everybody all stirred up. Any chance of slipping away with that treasure in the quiet of the night just evaporated. So now I'm having to resort to a more direct method of getting what I want."

The men forced Molly to sit on the floor as the van got under way. When she glanced into the rear of the cargo area, she spotted Lydia Crowe. Mascara-streaked tear tracks ran down her face.

"Ah, yes. Miss Crowe will be with us. I also offered to work something out with her brother regarding the treasure. He wasn't in an amenable mood. Pulled a gun on me is what he did. So I decided to give up on the treasure and find another way to make this a profitable trip for me. Between the ransom your husband pays for you and the one Aleister Crowe pays for his little sister, I'll bet I come out of this a wealthy man. What do you think, Mrs. Graham?"

"That you're vile and disgusting."

To her surprise, Draghici laughed. "Perhaps so, but soon I'll be a much richer, as well."

TROUBLED AND ANXIOUS, Michael sat in the quiet of his office and stared at the three-dimensional model of the clever puzzle Charles Crowe had designed.

The answers were there somewhere. He was sure of it. The frustration that they were practically within his grasp chafed at him unmercifully.

His mobile rang and showed Molly's picture. She was smiling at him, beautiful as ever. As he picked up the mobile, he noticed the time. She should have been home long before this, and he hadn't even noticed. That was definitely the sign of a bad husband.

"Hello, love."

"Michael."

At her frightened voice, he was instantly attentive. He sat forward in his chair, heart thumping. "Molly?"

"I'm all right, Michael. I feel like I'm in Xardon all over again, but I'm all right."

Xardon? As keyed up as he was, it took Michael a moment to remember that Xardon had been one of the adventure sites he'd created for "Makaum's Gauntlet," a fantasy pirate role-playing game. That had been one of Molly's favorites. But why had she brought it up?

"That's enough, missy." Draghici's rough voice was instantly recognizable.

Full-blown panic hit Michael.

"Mr. Graham."

"Yes."

"I know you're an intelligent man. Just a few days ago you stood on my boat and told me so in as many words. Now I'm prepared to tell *you* a few things."

Michael closed his eyes and forced himself to focus. Molly was alive. That was all that mattered right now. She was alive. He was going to find a way to keep her that way.

"Do you hear me, Mr. Graham?"

"Yes."

"You're not speaking much."

"What do you want me to say?"

Draghici chuckled. "Don't feel so high-and-mighty now, do you?"

Michael felt more afraid than he ever had in his life. His heart thundered so loud he could scarcely hear. "No."

"Good. See, I can invent games, too. And this is how we're going to play this one. If you tell anyone that I have your wife, anyone at all, you'll never see her again. You're going to wire two million dollars to an account I'm going to give you in the morning and you can have your wife back in one piece."

Michael didn't believe the man, but he didn't argue. It was just after eight o'clock now. He had about twelve hours to work with. Miracles could happen in that much time. "All right."

"I'll call you in the morning with the account number." The phone went dead.

Immediately, Michael pressed the speed-dial function and tried to call back. The mobile went directly to the answering service.

Don't panic. Breathe. Molly left you something. Why would she mention Xardon? He closed his eyes and remembered the game. Xardon had been a pirate empire along the coast. There, in the tunnels of the Windhollow Caves, the Blood Sails pirates had hidden their booty and taken refuge from their enemies.

Then Michael thought of the caves along Blackpool's coast and recalled the slave holding pens that had been mentioned in Nanny Myrie's ancestor's journal. He pulled up the PDF of the text on his computer and searched for mention of the pens.

According to the journal entries, the slaves had been kept underground beneath a cliff that overlooked shallows lined with sharp and jagged rocks. He consulted the topographical map he'd marked up, locating the opening where the slaves had been with grim certainty.

Satisfied he knew where Molly's "Xardon" was, he went to alert Iris and Irwin. What he was going to do, he was going to do alone, but he needed to have a backup.

He wasn't going to let Molly languish in Draghici's hands. He considered calling Paddington and telling the inspector of her kidnapping, but he immediately dismissed that. Michael felt certain that Draghici would follow through on his promise to kill Molly.

Even if Draghici didn't catch on to the fact that Paddington had been informed, Michael was afraid that Molly would be hurt in any police action to rescue her. If Draghici was where Michael believed he was, there were too many ways for the gypsy to escape, and Draghici probably knew most of them.

In order to get Molly out of harm's way, Michael knew he was going to have to push the gypsy leader into changing his plans. And the only way to do that was to step into the man's trap himself. If no one was left to pay the ransom, Draghici would have to take them into town to get the transfer done.

It was the best plan Michael could come up with on short notice, and he didn't want Molly to be in the clutches of those men by herself any longer than necessary.

The only other way was to somehow find Charles Crowe's elusive treasure for Draghici.

But before he threw himself into the fire, as well, he was going to tell two people about his mad plan to save Molly. Then, if something went wrong, Iris Dunstead and Irwin Jaeger could hopefully alert Paddington.

CHAPTER SEVENTEEN

MICHAEL WAS CERTAIN THE KIDNAPPERS saw him long before he stopped the powerboat and tossed the anchor over the side. He'd come in with the running lights on expressly so that he would be seen. Sneaking up on Draghici and the gypsies had seemed like a bad idea. Knowing that they were watching him made Michael afraid, but thinking of Molly in their hands terrified him. He tried not to imagine what she might have already suffered in the time the kidnappers had taken her.

He made himself focus on the task at hand. The shoreline under the rocky cliff lay a quarter-mile distant. He hadn't been able to get any closer because of the rocks hidden by the dark water. That was probably the reason Charles Crowe had chosen the location all those years ago. Moonlight skated along the foaming curlers pounding at the base of the cliff.

The shore existed in name only. There was nowhere else to go but up once he reached land. The cliff towered a hundred and fifty yards or more over the surf, and the nearly vertical climb would be brutal even if he'd been in his right mind and not worried about Molly.

He stripped off his sneakers and dropped them into the float bag he intended to bring with him, then pulled on a pair of swim fins. Undertow would be a problem.

If he couldn't make it to shore, the current would take him out to sea and no one would be left to save Molly.

He blew out a final breath and charged his lungs, then pulled on a snorkel and face mask. After clamping the mouthpiece between his teeth, he sat on the stern of the boat, tied the float bag to one of his ankles before tossing it overboard and flipped over backward into the sea.

The cold water leeched around his body and made him feel stiff at once. For a moment, he thought maybe he'd made a mistake trying to brave the water. Despite his wet suit, the cold alone felt as if it might kill him before he reached the beach. In one of his video games, a player character would probably give a little shiver, then settle into a natural stroke. But a player didn't actually feel the freezing bite. There was a big difference between the video-game environment and the real world.

Concentrating on Molly, telling himself she was still alive, Michael shut out the pain and uncertainty and swam. He pushed his body as if he was doing laps in a pool, staying with the motion, cutting through the waves. Water splashed continually across his face and streaked the view through the face mask, but he stayed focused on the shoreline every third or fourth stroke.

He was in good shape from rugby and other sports, and the activities he did around Blackpool kept him fit, as well. He took pride in that. But the swim was laborious and draining. His left thigh quivered with a minor cramp and he hoped it didn't flare up into full-blown agony. That would kill him, too. There were so many variables, all out of his control. His breath rushed out of him and back in when he turned his head, then he chopped through the sea again.

Gradually, taking much longer than he would have believed, Michael reached the abbreviated shore. The sharp edges of the rock cut through the wet suit and into his chest, stomach and legs as he clambered onto land. Chilled, his teeth chattering, he forced himself to a sitting position with his back to the cliff and slipped the fins off. He blew on his hands to warm them but they were still stiff as he unzipped his wet suit. The powerboat sitting at anchor looked impossibly far away. Michael knew he couldn't swim back.

James Bond and blokes like him made all this hero stuff look easy. Getting knocked about, chased and shot at was everyday business to that lot. Michael didn't like any of it. He'd rather have been home with a glass of wine, talking to Molly.

Except that Molly wasn't there.

Get a grip, mate. You've got a long way to go tonight if you're going to get her home safe.

He opened the bag and took out jeans, socks and the sneakers he'd put in there earlier, then pulled on a thermal undershirt, a rugby jersey and a thigh-length rain-resistant jacket. It wasn't spy gear, but it was warm. Then he started the torturous climb up the cliff face.

LESS THAN FIFTY FEET UP the steep incline, certain that he'd never make it to the top, not to mention the trip back down, Michael froze when a bright beam of a flashlight hit him. It was about bloody time. He'd been beginning to think he'd outfoxed himself.

He tried to follow the glare of the torch to its point of origin, but the brightness hurt his eyes too badly. When he blinked, spots danced in his vision.

"Mr. Graham."

"Yes." Michael sighed with relief and pulled himself in close to the rock face to better balance his weight. He didn't know how much strength he had left.

"To come out here, you're either a very brave man or a very stupid one."

"I'm alone, Draghici." The sharp stone dug into Michael's cheek and he felt his fingers slowly going numb with the cold.

"We saw your boat."

"I thought you would. That should also convince you I'm telling the truth about coming by myself."

"Provided you didn't inform Inspector Paddington of where you were off to."

"If I had, do you think he would have let me go through with this foolish idea? And I knew you would kill Molly if I allowed him to follow me."

Draghici was silent for a moment. "You do make a case for yourself."

Michael's fear abated a bit, but he wasn't out of the woods yet. "All I want is Molly. I want her safe."

"If you'd paid the ransom in the morning, you would have had her."

"I don't trust you."

Draghici laughed. "You trust me more while hanging to that wall like a fly?"

"You'll still get the ransom." Michael clung to the cliff with flagging strength. "It's set to be paid in the morning. But Molly and I have to be alive to validate the transaction. And we have to be safe." His arms and legs quaked with the strain. "If she's not in one piece, you won't get a penny."

"I'll still have you, Mr. Graham."

"No one will pay a ransom for me. I made certain

of that." Michael took a breath, his fingers burning as if they'd been set on fire. "If you don't let me climb to you—or climb down—I'm going to fall. I doubt I'll survive that."

"Prolly not. Hang on just a moment longer. Wouldn't want to miss out on a ransom."

The light retreated from Michael's face, but he was night blind now and still couldn't see anything. The only thing he could make out was that the light originated from a cave on the cliff face. He'd been close when he'd deduced where Charles Crowe's slave passageway was. He blinked his eyes but the effort wasn't helping very much.

"Mr. Graham?"

"Yes."

"I've got a lad coming out to you with a rope."

"Thank you." As soon as he said it, Michael realized how ridiculous it was to thank the man. If not for Draghici, he and Molly wouldn't be in any danger. At least, they wouldn't be in any danger from kidnappers. The secrets Michael had revealed were spreading fast. Many people, the Crowe family included, weren't going to be happy about that.

Breathing shallowly, concentrating on holding fast to the cliff, Michael watched as a slim man in a makeshift safety harness climbed out onto the wall. Draghici, or one of his clan, spotlighted handholds and footholds for him as he descended about ten feet and over a dozen to reach Michael.

"You ask me, you look about done in, mate." The gypsy crawled to a stop beside Michael.

"I am."

"My mates back there have got a rifle trained on you.

Just so's that's plain enough. You do anything untoward, they're gonna shoot you through the head and we'll toss your body in the water. We'll drop the missus in after you."

"Got it." Michael's legs and arms trembled violently. He hated the man, hated the power Draghici had over Molly and him. "I'm not going to be able to hang on long."

"First thing I'm gonna do is pat you down, make sure you ain't carrying no gun or nothing."

"Waste of time. I'm not."

"My time to waste, isn't it?"

Desperately, Michael clung to the rock while the gypsy ran hands over his chest, belt, arms and legs. He even pulled up Michael's pants to clear his sneakers, and almost dislodged Michael in the process. He took Michael's mobile and his wallet, pocketing both.

The man pulled back a little and raised his voice. "He's clean. Nothin' on him."

"Then bring him back over here."

"Aye." The gypsy leaned back to Michael. "Got a rope here I'm gonna fashion you a harness out of. You've come this far, don't want to lose you now."

"Okay." Michael braced himself and moved slightly as Draghici's goon ran the rope around him and expertly tied it in a makeshift climbing rig. The bloody thing was painfully tight over his crotch, but it seemed as if it would hold. Then the man tied another rope to the halter.

"My mates are on the other end of that one. They're gonna pull slow and easy, take some of the weight off you."

Michael nodded.

"First thing, don't try to climb. Go straight across till you're beneath them. Less chance of you falling that way. Once you're under them, they can help haul you up."

"All right."

"Get on with yourself, then." The gypsy cupped his hands around his mouth and spoke louder. "He's coming. Stand steady."

Fingers numb but aching deep in the joints, Michael carefully made his way across the cliff face. As he neared the cave, more and more of his weight was taken on the rope. Once he was below the cave, he started up. Draghici's man had all of his weight on the rope and the only thing he had to do was keep his face from getting turned into hamburger against the cliff.

As Michael climbed over the lip of the cave, Draghici stood there, smiling down at him. The gypsy leader held a kerosene lantern in one hand.

"You're a proper twonk, Mr. Graham."

Weakly, Michael flopped over onto his back and stared up at Draghici. His legs hurt too much to take his weight, and he honestly thought he might never walk again. The cold, hard ground felt amazingly reassuring. "You'll get no argument from me."

"Had a lookout here in the cave mouth because I figured your little wife might have gotten a message to you. Didn't have no such worries about the Crowe woman. But you and your missus, you're too clever by half."

Crowe woman?

"Molly didn't tell me anything." No matter what happened, Michael didn't want Draghici angry at her. "I figured you had to have a place to hide your prisoners. You know a lot about Charles Crowe and his slave trade. It seemed reasonable that you might use this place."

Draghici knelt down beside Michael. The gypsy leader grinned good-naturedly. "See? Too clever by half. And you're sure Paddington doesn't have any idea about this entrance?"

"No, he doesn't."

"How did you come to learn of it?" Draghici fisted Michael's jacket in one hand and hauled him to his feet.

Michael stood on jelly legs. Only part of his infirmity came from the climb and the swim. "Does it matter? I'm here. How did you know about Charles Crowe's secret enterprise?"

Draghici smiled. "The Romany forget nothing. After he stole my ancestor's gold, it was the mission of every member of the clan to retrieve our fortune and our honor. Stories passed down through the generations speak of the men of our clan who infiltrated Crowe's operation to learn of the gold's location and to bring the traitor down. They were able to leak information to the Royal Navy's West Africa Squadron, but no trace of the gold was ever found. And so, generation after generation, our search continued, including my grandfather, my father and now me, passing down all the information we had learned."

He directed the lantern light to the floor at the edge of the cave mouth and a shape carved into the rock emerged from the shadows. It was a square about four inches across.

"Do you know what that is, Mr. Graham?"

"A symbol Charles Crowe had etched into the tunnels to guide his men." Michael had seen the markings on the map he'd gotten from the puzzle cube and now felt certain they could be nothing else. He just didn't understand the riddle behind them.

"That's right. Many of the people involved in the slave trade couldn't read or write English. Handy for my ancestors, too."

Draghici moved the lantern from the wall to the dark throat of the tunnel. "These symbols are a simple language that Crowe's guards could read." He shone the lamp on the square again. "These squares mark paths to the slave holding pens he carved out of the rocks." He motioned the light forward. "Let's go, Mr. Graham. Time's a-wasting."

CHAPTER EIGHTEEN

IN ALL HIS STUDIES and research about the practice of slavery, Michael had only guessed what it might be like to feel helpless in enemy hands. With his imagination, he'd even used the conceit of being trapped in a few video games. In the games, the characters were always looking for clues and a means of escape. They remained brave and steadfast.

Being brave and steadfast in the face of certain death, as it turned out, was no easy matter. Not even when he had an escape plan. He hoped it would work, but he hadn't counted on Draghici having so many men at his disposal.

Michael walked through the narrow tunnel and felt the same desperation and sense of doom Crowe's illegal cargo must have surely felt. There was no escape through the solid stone that surrounded him. He closed his eyes for a moment and searched through the images he'd memorized of the underground labyrinth on the bottom of the cube, certain that map revealed something about the path he was currently walking.

Come on, mate. You're good at memory games. You've got a photographic memory when it comes to stuff like this. But even games that had built-in map features didn't help when a player was trying to avoid death.

As he walked, he counted his steps, keeping track of the twists and turns as they went deeper into the cliff.

"Do you think Crowe truly left a treasure out there?" Draghici walked at Michael's side.

Michael hesitated, wondering how to best answer him. What did the gypsy leader want to hear? That was the real question. "I don't know. What do you think?"

"Personally, I've lately come to believe those stories are all a load of rot. I'm of the opinion that whatever Crowe might have gotten from my people was spent before he died or else found long ago." Draghici waved at the passageway. "Look around you. Would a rich man continue to traffic in slaves when it was illegal?"

"If he wanted more money, yes."

"Is that what it was about? Greed?"

"Crowe wasn't operating a charity. He was making a profit."

"Seems like a bloke would have enough after a while. By all accounts, he was a wealthy man. Why take the risk?"

"Why risk kidnapping someone?"

Draghici laughed and the hollow echo rolled before them, sounding as evil as anything Michael had ever heard. "Me and my family are different than Charles Crowe. We haven't already made our fortunes."

"Yeah."

"I have to admit, for a while there I was pulling for you."

"What do you mean?"

"I thought if anyone was to find the treasure, it would be you."

"Sorry to disappoint."

Draghici shrugged. "No, actually, you didn't disappoint. Stealing the treasure once it was discovered was Plan A. Kidnapping Lydia Crowe was Plan B. Plan B is still working, and now we've got the added bonus of ransoming you and your wife."

Lydia? That was the "Crowe woman" Draghici had mentioned earlier? A second kidnapping victim changed everything. He'd counted on rescuing Molly, but two women would make it a great deal harder.

The lantern light touched a rusty iron door set into the rock wall. Iron bars crossed a narrow window. A young man stood to one side of the door, and a group huddled farther away, talking quietly. He had a big pistol holstered at his hip and the white cord of earphones crossed his chest.

"Watching you fail at finding the treasure just helped me get over hoping it existed. If it hadn't been for you, I might have hung around this town for years for nothing. Now I can make a tidy profit and escape with a whole skin. I can live with that."

On the opposite side of this tunnel, the black mouth of another yawned. Michael caught a glimpse of the symbol carved into the floor—another square. He took a deep breath and let it out slowly.

Growling a curse, Draghici stepped forward and back-handed the guard in the face. The man staggered back and swore, putting a hand to his bloody lips.

"Why did you do that?"

Draghici pulled the earphone cords and popped the buds out of the man's ears. "When you're on guard duty, Anton, you're supposed to be listening, as well as watching."

"I'd notice the door opening, wouldn't I? And it ain't like nobody's gonna get down this far. It's boring standing here for hours. A blind man could keep watch over those two birds. You didn't have to hit me."

"I'll hit you again if I've a mind to. And if I catch you listening to that thing again, I'll beat you half to death. You understand me?"

Sullenly, the guard put his earphones into his pocket and stepped to one side. Blood speckled his chin. "Sure, mate. I understand."

"Get this bloody door open."

Anton hauled a long iron key from his pocket and stepped toward the lock.

"Where did you find the key?" Michael couldn't stop himself from asking.

"My father found it years ago. After some searching, he discovered it fit in the slave holding pens. Took a bit of oil to get it working, but these locks were made to last." Draghici shifted the lantern and pointed out an iron spike that someone had driven into the wall. "A lot of the stuff in the slavery pens hadn't been touched since old Charles Crowe had his business up and running."

"Can I see that key?"

Draghici considered for a moment, then nodded to the guard, who handed over the key. Draghici shone his lantern on it. Michael examined the key and scratched a thumbnail over the engravings at the end.

"What are you thinking?"

"Do you see these markings on the bow?"

"What bow?" The gypsy guard leaned in closer. "Ain't no bow on there, mate."

"The bow is the flat part of the key after the blade. The part you use to turn it with."

The guard grunted but didn't sound impressed.

Draghici, however, was captivated. "What about those

markings? That's a square. Means it's for this door." He shone the lantern on the engraving of a square above the rusty door.

Michael rubbed at the key some more. "Was this a triangle? The key is so worn, I'm not sure. But it looks like a triangle."

"Let me see that." Draghici plucked the key from Michael's fingers and scratched at the key himself. "Could be a triangle. What of it?"

"Are there any other doors nearby?"

Draghici closed his fist around the key. "There are."

"Are there any you haven't been able to open?"

"No."

"Okay. Probably nothing, then."

"What's 'probably nothing'?"

Michael struggled to pull off a theatrical pause when all he wanted to do was blurt out the false lead he'd thought of on the spot. "Just me imagining things. That's not a triangle."

Draghici squared up with him, looking even more deadly. "If you've got something on your mind, mate, I want to know it. It would go easier on you if I didn't have to beat it out of you."

Spin the story, Michael. That's what you're good at. Don't tell the whole thing. Just give him enough to let him think he's figured out the answer on his own. That was one of a storyteller's best gifts: intriguing an audience just enough to get them to do at least half the work and provide an equal amount of excitement.

"How much of this area have you searched?"

Draghici hesitated. "A lot of it over the years."

"But not all?"

"There are a lot of caves and tunnels down here. Regular rat's nest."

"I know. I found a map of the tunnels."

Draghici's eyes narrowed and he leaned in closer to Michael. His men took a step forward, as well. All the lanterns and torches were focused on Michael. "You found a map?"

"Yes. I replicated Charles Crowe's model of the town and discovered it was a map."

One of the gypsies in the back spoke up in hushed tones. "It must lead to the treasure! The gold could still be down here somewhere."

The other gypsies started talking at the same time.

"Quiet!" Draghici's roar pealed off the tunnel walls.

Instantly, the men fell silent.

Excitement burned in Draghici's gaze.

Michael both saw and felt it, and he intended to make the most of it.

"You need to keep talking, Mr. Graham."

"I was just wondering about that key." Michael rubbed his jaw, as if he was just putting the pieces together. Which he was. He was weaving the story as he told it. That was what he did best, drawing on information close at hand as well as things he already knew. He also played on the expectations of his audience.

"Thinking it might open more than just this door," Draghici suggested.

"Yeah. Maybe that key belonged to one of Charles Crowe's jailers, and maybe that man had other responsibilities besides keeping the slaves under lock and key."

Draghici held up the key and waved it thoughtfully.

"Perhaps this key opens more than just doors." He smiled, obviously taken with his own cleverness.

Shaking his head, knowing he had the man firmly hooked, Michael looked around the passage. "You're just getting your hopes up. I don't think this section of the tunnels was on the map. The treasure probably isn't out here."

"You let me be the judge of that."

Michael focused on the man and played devil's advocate. "Crowe would never have buried the treasure so far away from him. He'd have kept it somewhere close. So he could go visit it anytime he wanted to."

"This isn't one of those video games you write. A man wanting to hide something, he's gonna conceal it where no one can find it. Where he can get at it without no one being the wiser. Look at where Crowe hid those slaves. We're three miles away from the town. Even back in those days, a carriage could have brought him out here easy and quick enough. A fast horse would have brought him even sooner."

"You can't move a treasure trove on a single horse."

"You don't have to move all of it at once. You take just a little at a time. You're limiting yourself by assuming Charles Crowe would want to move it all."

Michael shook his head. "I don't think the treasure exists. It's just a story."

"He's lying to us." Anton shoved his torch into Michael's face. "He figures he can pay the ransom for himself and his wife, then come back here and find that treasure. Make himself even richer than he already is, while we settle for peanuts."

A few of the other gypsies echoed that sentiment.

The guard punched Michael in the chest. "Get that

pretty wife of his out here and put a gun to her head. Either he tells us what he knows or we blow her head off."

In that moment, Michael despised Anton in spite of the sympathies he'd felt for the young man when Draghici had hit him.

"Is that what we should do?" The gypsy leader plucked the pistol from his belt. "Easy enough if we wanted to."

Realizing he was flirting with disaster, Michael looked directly into Draghici's greedy gaze and told the truth. "If I knew the location of Charles Crowe's treasure, I would have revealed it already to keep my wife safe. You wouldn't have to threaten her."

Draghici held Michael's gaze for a long moment, then nodded. "I believe you."

Michael relaxed a little but the blood still pounded in his ears.

"But I think you gave up on finding the treasure too soon." Draghici smiled smugly. "You figured out the meaning of the symbols Crowe used to mark his passages?"

"Yes." That was a bit of a bluff, but Michael had to make the decision immediately. If the gypsy knew about the square symbol, it only stood to reason that he would know about the others, as well.

"Crowe used four of them," Draghici explained. "The triangle, square, pentagon and the hexagon. Each one of those symbols related to some aspect of Crowe's travels through these tunnels. He used triangles to mark his supply areas. Squares for the slave pen areas. Pentagons for hidden tunnels. And hexagons for traps."

Michael filed away the information. Draghici had

more knowledge of the cave system Charles Crowe had designed than Michael did. For all his cleverness, though, the gypsy leader had missed two symbols—the single line and two parallel lines. Those had been marked on Crowe's map and were obviously important.

Draghici touched his nose. "Somewhere in this unexplored area, Crowe left the gold he stole from my family."

"I think you're wasting your time." Michael pointed out the time factor so Draghici would put pressure on himself.

The gypsy leader glanced at his watch. "Eleven-twenty. We've got a few hours yet before morning. Anton, lock Mr. Graham in the cell. We've got us a bit of hunting to do."

Draghici used the key to unlock the cell door and swung it open. Anton grabbed Michael by the arm and shoved him into the room. At first he thought he'd been tricked, that Draghici hadn't locked him up with Molly. Then he heard her voice whisper softly out of the darkness.

"Michael?"

CHAPTER NINETEEN

"Hello, love."

Molly stepped toward her husband's voice and couldn't believe his tone. She recognized that undercurrent of emotion and knew that he thought he'd just accomplished something incredibly brilliant with no one the wiser.

But she heard the fear in his words, too. That feeling resonated within her as she reached for his shadow, barely outlined by the lantern light behind him. Then his arms were around her and she welcomed the solid heat of him.

"A bit of a pickle we're in, isn't it? Where's Lydia?"

"Over in the corner. She passed out. What are you doing here?"

"Couldn't very well let my best girl go it alone, now could I?"

"Yes, you could. You should be at home where it's safe."

"I missed you."

For a moment, Molly was torn between holding him tighter and yelling at him. One of the things that had gotten her through the past hours was knowing that Michael was safe. Or rather, *believing* that he was safe.

And now both their lives were at risk. Guilt stung her when she realized she felt so relieved that he was with her. He should have been far away.

Reluctantly, Molly let go of Michael and got control of herself. Michael trailed his fingers over her arms, not wanting to lose her again.

"Tell me you brought help."

"Just me and my ingenuity. Anything else might have proven disastrous."

"Coming here is disastrous."

Michael took her hands and kissed her fingers. "Doesn't even compare to finding out you'd been kidnapped, love. Trust me on that."

"You were supposed to pay the ransom in the morning."

"I'd rather we not hang about that long if we can help it."

Barely any light filtered in through the iron-barred window in the door. Molly had to look at things indirectly to see them. Michael had taught her to do that when they walked in the dark during camping excursions. "We don't have a choice."

"I'm hoping we do."

Though she could barely see Michael, she could tell he was slipping his pants down. "What are you doing?"

"I was counting on Draghici and his mates not being overly cautious when they frisked me. They were looking for weapons. I brought these." Michael pulled his pants back up and held out something in one hand.

"What?"

"Lock picks."

"You brought lock picks?"

"Don't talk so disparagingly of them. I had to tape them to the inside of my thigh to prevent them from being found. It's not exactly been the most comfortable few minutes."

Despite the gravity of the situation, Molly couldn't help chuckling.

"Now, there you go. No respect for my ingenuity." Michael retreated to the door and peered out.

"How did you get here? What are you doing?" Lydia Crowe's voice, tense and scratchy from crying, came out of the corner.

"I came to rescue you." Michael waved Molly over.

"Rescue?" Lydia's voice grew more shrill. "If we try to escape, they'll kill us. I'm not going to let you endanger us." She stepped closer, and the light lifted her out of the blackness.

Michael turned quickly and grabbed Lydia by the shoulders. "You keep yourself together, Miss Crowe. I didn't come out here to lose my wife."

Lydia struggled against him, but Michael held on. "Guard!" She tried to yell again, but Michael clapped a hand over her mouth and looked desperately at Molly.

Outside the door, the young gypsy stood in the same position he'd been in for the past few hours. He wore his earbuds again and the volume was turned up loud enough that Molly could faintly hear it. The tune wasn't one Molly wanted as the last song she heard before she died.

"He's listening to his music. The others must have gone with Draghici to search the tunnels."

Michael relaxed a little, but he didn't release Lydia.

Molly walked back to the young woman. Lydia's eyes were round with terror. "You listen to me. Right now. Even if your brother paid the ransom, these men aren't going to release us. We're witnesses. We know their faces. We can identify them. As soon as they have their money, they'll kill us." Saying it aloud like that, even though she'd been thinking it for hours, made Molly tremble. She took a short breath and focused on the here and now. "Do you understand?"

Tears filled Lydia's eyes and spilled down her cheeks. She nodded.

"Now, when Michael lets go of you, you won't scream."

Lydia shook her head.

"We haven't even gotten out of this cell. Draghici won't allow his men to hurt us until he gets the money or believes he's not going to get it."

Lydia nodded.

"All right, Michael."

Slowly, Michael took his hand away from the young woman's face. Lydia shivered, her breath coming in wet gulps, but she didn't cry out.

"That's good." Michael's voice was calm. "Just stay with us and we'll all get out of here. Wait and see."

Lydia nodded again, then retreated to the back wall and sat in the darkness. The light hardly touched her and she almost disappeared in a way Molly found eerie.

"Thank you for getting her to calm down." Michael returned to the door, checked on the guard, then set to work with the lock picks.

"Staying calm is hard."

"Be a love and keep watch over that bloke, would you? I wouldn't want him catching me in the middle of this."

Molly joined Michael at the door and peered through the bars. The young gypsy was really giving himself over to the music, jerking his whole body to the rhythm. Every now and again, he threw out an arm or a leg in an improvised dance step.

"It's really sad, isn't it?" Michael maneuvered his picks with deliberation.

"I thought you said Keith taught you how to pick locks."

Michael looked up at her. "Don't take your eyes off the guard."

Chastened, Molly watched the man. "Sorry."

"No problem. I've almost got it. So, no, this lock isn't sad. It's quite easy. But that man's dancing ability is atrocious."

"I don't know how you can make jokes at a time like this."

"Well, there's an improvement."

"What do you mean?"

"Usually you don't let me tell jokes at all."

"Your timing isn't appropriate, Michael."

"I talk when I'm nervous. I've a right to be nervous now." Michael leaned back. "Got it."

Molly's heart leaped in her chest. The guard had a weapon and she didn't doubt that he would use it if he felt he had to. He was also as tall as Michael and a little heavier. She glanced back but couldn't see Lydia in the darkness.

"When we get out there, grab his torch. We're going to need it." Michael stood and put his lock picks into his pocket.

"What are you going to grab?"

"His mobile if he has one. They took mine."

Lydia spoke up quietly. "There's no signal down here."

"I figured as much, but once we get aboveground, we might be able to catch a signal long enough to call in Paddington and his blokes. We can follow the tunnels.

We'll find a way out. Even wandering around in the dark is better than being locked up." Michael looked at them. "Stay back until I have this situation under control, Molly."

"Be careful."

Slowly, Michael opened the door. Since the lantern was outside, his shadow stayed inside the room as he reached for the man. Quicker than Molly would have thought possible, and more merciless than she'd ever seen her husband before, Michael grabbed the guard from behind, wrapping his hand over the man's face. The guard had just a moment to react, then Michael slammed the back of his head against the stone wall.

The young gypsy slumped to the floor, and for a moment Molly stood there, frozen. Michael seemed spellbound, as well, gazing down on him with a mixture of horror, fear and anger.

Molly brushed by Michael and captured the lantern. She placed her fingers over the man's neck.

"Is he…?" Michael couldn't go any further.

"He's alive."

"Thank God." For an instant he looked as if he was going to be sick. Then he gave himself a shake, took a deep breath and knelt down beside the unconscious man.

Molly watched her husband with new eyes. She'd always known Michael Graham was a brave man, and a tender one, too. But to see his reaction to the violence he'd committed, his regret, made her realize even more how much she loved him. He wasn't a professional soldier carrying out an action he'd become used to. He was a man out of his depth, protecting his own and regretting what he had to do.

With trembling hands, Michael searched the man's pockets. "No mobile."

Molly stood and peered down the hallway. "Which way?"

"If we can't find another way out, we'll go back to the cliff. We can swim if we have to."

Lydia walked out of the cell, eyes fixated on the guard, her arms wrapped around her torso. "I can't swim."

"You can't?" Michael stared at her in disbelief.

"No."

"It'll be all right." Molly slipped her an arm around the young woman. "You didn't bring a life jacket, did you, Michael?"

"I thought that might look a tad suspicious." He sighed and peered down the tunnel.

Lydia raised her head. "The two of you can go on. Leave me behind."

"Well, that wouldn't be a very successful rescue, now would it?" Michael tried to smile, but the tension in his expression told Molly he was worried. "Charles Crowe had to have a quick route between Blackpool and his ships. That tunnel must be close by. Or at least one that leads us away from Draghici's clan."

"There are a lot of tunnels down here." Molly knelt by the unconscious guard and started going through his pockets.

"I didn't find a mobile, love."

"What about a map? They'd need to know how to get to and from Blackpool." Molly turned the man's pockets inside out. Coins, revolver rounds, paper money and a cherry-flavored lip balm tumbled to the worn stone floor.

That gave Michael pause and he grimaced. "Good

idea." He dropped down on the guard's other side. "With the maze of tunnels down here, it would stand to reason that they don't have them all memorized, now wouldn't it?"

"Yes."

Voices and footsteps echoed through the tunnel, coming closer. "I'm telling you, I think Graham knows more than he's saying. That bloke is lying about the treasure. I can see it in his eyes."

Michael grimaced. "Apparently the little snipe hunt I convinced them to go on isn't nearly as consuming as I'd hoped. We need to get moving." He picked up the man's iPod and earbuds, then shoved them into a pocket. After a brief hesitation, he picked up the guard's revolver, as well.

"Michael."

He shook his head. "I don't intend to play nice, Molly. Not after everything we've been through."

Molly didn't have time to ask him why he took the iPod. Michael grabbed Lydia by the elbow and hurried her forward. Then he gripped Molly's arm and pulled her along.

"C'mon. You've got the light."

Molly took the lead. Her muscles were stiff and cramped from sitting in the underground prison so long. She tried not to dwell on what would happen if Draghici and his men overtook them. Quietly, Michael called out the turns while matching stride with Lydia. He kept his free hand on the young woman and propelled her forward. Molly knew he was calling the turns out from his memory of when Draghici had brought him to the prison cell. He had a phenomenal memory.

After a final left turn, Molly stared down at the mouth

of the tunnel where a man stood smoking a cigarette, a rifle slung over his shoulder. He noticed the light at once, though he hadn't made out her features.

"Hey. Be a mate and bring me a sandwich. It's been hours since I've had anything to eat."

Molly kept the light pointed ahead of her to partially blind the man, but she didn't have the voice to pull it off.

"Sure. Give me a minute and I'll get it for you." Michael pulled Molly's elbow and he lowered his voice. "Not this way. His rifle will cut us to pieces."

Molly kept the flashlight pointed away from them so the man wouldn't realize they weren't his friends. Once she rounded the corner, she took the lead again and shone the light ahead of them.

They passed several doors, and Michael tried them all. Unfortunately, the only ones that opened were holding pens like the one they'd come from.

"Hey!" The shout splintered the relative silence that had filled the tunnels. "Anton's down! The prisoners have escaped!"

Michael frowned. "Well, the cat's out of the bag now."

"Somebody get Draghici!"

Michael pointed forward. "To your left, Molly. Take the tunnel."

She did as he directed, lighting their way down another passage.

"I need to look at the marking on the floor," Michael said.

When she directed the light toward the ground where the two tunnels met, she discovered that the one they were in was marked with a square. The other hallway was marked with a triangle.

"You're going to have to help me keep these straight if I'm going to memorize them." Michael nudged her forward. "Otherwise we're going to end up even more lost."

"Square leads to triangle. Got it." Molly wondered which would be worse: getting caught by Draghici and his men, or ending up wandering around in the tunnels, utterly lost. The batteries would last only a few hours, if that. The prospect of being stranded in the dark was immediately frightening.

"Don't worry, love. This cave system is a natural maze. If there's one thing I'm good at, it's mazes."

CHAPTER TWENTY

AS HE TRAILED AFTER MOLLY down the new tunnel, Michael remained uncomfortably aware of the revolver's solid weight in his hand. The mechanics of the weapon would be no problem. He'd shot a gun before, as research for games. He had good aim according to the ex–Special Boat Services man that had taught him the difference between semiautomatic pistols and revolvers. But Michael was uneasy around guns. While he enjoyed shooting paper targets at the range, the thought of what a bullet could do to a flesh-and-blood human being was something else.

He'd seen a few dead bodies since coming to Blackpool and the images often haunted Michael at night.

Are you prepared to do it, mate? Can you kill someone? He didn't want to think that he could, but if Molly's life was on the line, he would.

That certainty brought him no comfort.

The gypsies continued to yell and curse behind them. A full-fledged search was under way.

"DID I EVER TELL YOU HOW I spent three full days lost in the Misty Corners of Drable in Dark God's Catacombs?" Molly couldn't believe she was talking, and was embarrassed by the fear she heard in her own voice.

"No."

"That was before I met you and knew you'd designed that level of the game, but I hated you for those three days."

"A lot of people did while they were in Misty Corners, but they felt quite the opposite when they finally got through." Michael watched the walls, looking for any indication that would tell him where they were, she assumed. For as much as she knew, they were headed *away* from Blackpool, not toward it.

"How did Draghici find this place?" she asked.

"Hand-me-down stories from his ancestors."

Molly shone her light at the next juncture. "Which way?"

"Take the first."

Three corners later, Molly swept the torch over an area with two connecting tunnels in addition to the right-hand turn. She couldn't fathom how Michael could be memorizing them all, but she was certain that he was. "There are *two* left turns this time."

"Pick one, and if you come up to a door configuration like this again, keep choosing the same doorway. At least this path seems to be taking us away from where we've been."

Molly walked into the tunnel and hurried ahead. The light bounced before her and she kept watch for any lights approaching from the opposite direction. The fear that she'd run upon someone hiding in the darkness haunted her.

Gradually, the tunnel grew larger. The stink of brine hung in the air. On another day, standing on the deck of their boat with the sun overhead, Molly would have enjoyed the smell. But not now.

The sudden descent almost tripped her up. Before

Michael could reach for her, she caught herself by slamming a hand into the wall. The flashlight banged against the stone, as well, going dark for a few moments.

The flashlight's beam suddenly expanded in front of Molly and disappeared. Startled, she stopped so quickly that Lydia ran into her and nearly knocked her down. Michael hauled Lydia up while Molly managed on her own.

She shone the light around the vast space in front of them. "This is a cave." Water lapped at an irregular shoreline only a short distance in front of them. Something metallic gleamed briefly in the darkness.

"This is a dead end," Molly said. "We're going to have to go back."

Michael released Lydia and stepped forward. "Put the torch more to the right. I thought I saw something there."

When the beam of light shifted, it revealed the bow of a powerboat sitting at anchor in the cave's natural harbor.

In front of them, a rickety wooden pier ran out a dozen feet into the water. As the boat floated, it bumped up against the pier hard enough to make it vibrate.

Michael scanned the deck warily for signs of any of Draghici's men as he brought the pistol up. Lydia stepped back.

No one was aboard the boat.

Michael let the pistol fall to his side again. "Well, we know how Draghici and his men got here."

Behind the boat, a broad, low cave mouth opened out into the sea. Wind blew through the gap and brought a chill that bit at Michael's nose and ears. Lydia wrapped her arms around herself and his heart went out to her, but there was nothing he could do.

He held out his hand to Molly. "Might I borrow the torch?"

"I'll come with you."

"Molly, one of Draghici's men could be on that boat."

"If so, you'll need both hands to deal with him."

Reluctantly, knowing he was in for a fight they could ill afford to have at the moment, Michael nodded. "Together, then." With Molly to his left and slightly behind him, they went forward. The wood of the pier was rotted and broken, shivering under their weight, and he worried that it would give way beneath them before they reached the boat.

Let the keys be in it. Let the keys be in it. Michael kept up the silent mantra till he threw a leg over the side and Molly directed the torchlight over the controls.

There were no keys.

Thankfully there was no one aboard, either.

"I don't suppose Keith taught you how to hot-wire a boat."

Michael unclipped a torch from beside the steering wheel and grabbed a couple of nylon jackets that would at least protect against the wind. "Keith's not really a boat person." He clicked the torch on and shone it around the deck. "Take a look. What else we can salvage."

A rifle hung in the cabin and Michael was sorely tempted to take it. Draghici's gypsies probably used it to fend off sharks, but he figured the weapon would be too unwieldy in the caves. Besides, he wasn't a sniper by any stretch of the imagination. Shooting a man in cold blood was something he was sure he couldn't do. He'd use the revolver only in close quarters if he absolutely had to.

Still, he couldn't leave the rifle for Draghici and his men. He heaved the weapon over the side and it sank into the water like a rock.

"Here's an emergency kit." Molly hauled her prize up and set it on the stern seats.

The red steel box looked promising, but it turned out not to hold much. Michael had to admit that finding a police radio or a helicopter, even the keys, inside would have been too much to expect.

Waves lapped at the boat's hull as he and Molly sorted through everything in the cabin. They kept the flare gun and three rounds, a roll of duct tape, a fishing knife and a Leatherman multitool.

Molly also took half a dozen energy bars and five water bottles she found in an ice chest. "Lydia and I missed dinner."

"I don't have enough pockets for everything." Michael glanced around.

"You could always duct tape everything to you."

"Now who's being inappropriately funny?"

Molly opened more seat compartments and brought out a vinyl rucksack. "This?"

"Will work beautifully." Michael took the rucksack and stuffed the items into it while she pulled on one of the windbreakers.

"I've also got more batteries for the flashlights. I mean, the torches."

Michael grinned and kissed her. "I knew what you meant. I've given up hope that you'll ever speak the Queen's English the way it's meant to be spoken." He added the batteries to the rucksack.

"Someone's coming!" Lydia called from the shoreline.

Looking toward the tunnel they'd just left, Michael saw that light was filling the space. "Time to go."

"Where?"

Scanning the cave, he discovered the cave had precious few hiding places, and none of them good. Hiding on the boat would only get them recaptured in short order.

"I think I see another tunnel." Molly aimed her torch at the wall on the opposite side of the cave, about forty yards away. "Isn't that a trail?"

Staring hard, Michael barely made out the worn path. "It is. Good eyes. Let's go." He climbed out of the boat and gave Molly a hand up. Then they ran down the swaying pier to Lydia.

The young woman held her hands up in front of her. She was shaking and nearly frantic. "They're going to kill us."

"Not yet." Michael helped her into the other jacket he'd found, then grabbed her arm and followed Molly as she ran along the narrow U-shaped trail that bordered the miniature harbor.

The light in the other tunnel grew steadily brighter. They were almost at the mouth of the second entrance when Draghici's gypsies poured into the harbor cave.

"There they are!"

Harsh thunder cracks crescendoed through the cavern. Bullets tore sparks from the wall around Michael. He watched over Molly, willing her not to be injured.

"Stop shooting, Mihai, you bloody fool!"

Silence fell.

"If you kill them before Draghici tells you to, he'll

tie a boat anchor around your feet and dump you into the sea."

Breath burning his throat and his heart pounding, Michael guided Lydia into the tunnel after Molly. The gunshots still echoed in his ears. Glancing over his shoulder, he spotted three torches careening down the incline toward the water. There were more men than he'd thought.

He turned his back to the harbor and concentrated on running for his life.

"MICHAEL, THERE ARE TWO tunnels ahead." Molly's torch cast a broad arc. "I'm going to stay to the right."

"Sounds fine."

Lydia staggered and almost fell, kept vertical only by Michael's quick reflexes. She was flagging, almost out of breath. She wouldn't be able to maintain this pace.

"This is stupid." Lydia gasped for air. "We don't know where we're going."

Michael kept hold of her elbow and tried to support her as much as he could. "We're heading in the opposite direction from Draghici and his goons. For the moment, I'll count that as a win. As for where we're going, that harbor back there gave us a clue."

"How?"

"The cave mouth faced the sea, and the sea is to the east of Blackpool. We had to cross the harbor to get here, which means we're headed south toward Blackpool."

"I hope you're right."

"I am. Just keep moving."

"I'll try."

Molly entered the tunnel on the right and Michael followed.

A HANDFUL OF TURNS LATER, Lydia started retching. Michael watched, feeling sorry for her, but there was nothing he could do. The pace he and Molly set was brutal to someone who didn't work out regularly. Luckily Lydia had been able to keep up long enough to get them away from Draghici's thugs.

"I'm sorry. I'm sorry." Lydia's voice was plaintive.

"You're doing fine." Molly lifted her hands behind her head to open her lungs more. "Put your hands behind your head like this. It'll help you recover more quickly."

While Molly coached Lydia and kept her from panicking, Michael studied the tunnel and noticed a new opening in the side wall. He turned his torchlight onto the floor and looked for the engravings he knew had to be there.

A single line showed.

He knelt and brushed at it, making sure there wasn't a second line beside the first. He still wasn't certain of the significance of the six symbols he'd found on the model he and Rohan had put together. In their haste to escape their pursuers, he hadn't been able to get a close view of the symbols as they'd rushed through the intersections. But his subconscious had hold of something and was worrying at whatever it was like a terrier.

It floated at the back of his mind, tantalizingly just out of reach.

Voices echoed in the tunnel, coming closer again. He returned to Molly and Lydia. "Can you go on?" he asked Lydia.

"I don't have a choice, do I?" She heaved herself off the wall and they hurried on.

CHAPTER TWENTY-ONE

AFTER ANOTHER INTERSECTION with three tunnels and two turns, Michael thought it was safe enough for them to rest. They made a jog to the left that kept them hidden and switched off the torches.

Hearing the men slog past their hiding spot was unnerving, but when one of them shone a torch into the tunnel, Michael held the revolver in his hand and swallowed hard. He was certain he was going to have to shoot someone.

Then the man pulled back and rejoined his mates without ever seeing their quarry. Within a few minutes, their footsteps retreated.

Molly clicked on her torch and aimed the beam at the ceiling so the light reflected back down and lit up the small area they'd claimed as their hiding spot. She looked tired.

Michael reached into the rucksack and brought out the energy bars. "Can you eat?"

"I'm starving." Molly reached for one.

Lydia didn't say anything.

Taking another bar, Molly proffered it to the young woman. "You need to eat."

"I can't. I'll just throw it up."

"Maybe it'll calm you down. At the very least, the

sugar will give you some extra energy over the next hour or so. Try it."

Without enthusiasm, Lydia did as she was told. She unwrapped the bar and started to throw the wrapper to the ground.

Michael held out a hand. "Here. Let me have that. If we leave a trail behind, Draghici's men will find it." When Lydia passed the wrapper over to him, he shoved it into his pants pocket.

Both women ate, then drank sparingly from the water bottles. Michael searched the tunnel ahead of them and noticed a small incline. That made him hopeful because it meant they were getting close to the surface again. That had to be good.

He returned to the women. "Ready?"

"Yes." Molly tucked the water bottles into the rucksack.

Michael slung the bag into position and took up the lead. Senses alert, he heard only the sound of his beating heart and their shoes scuffing across the stone. Then he noticed something else. "Do you smell that?"

"What?"

"Grass, if I'm not mistaken."

Molly sniffed the air, then nodded. "It *is* grass."

"Means we're almost there!" Increasing his stride, Michael pushed forward. He probed the dark ceiling with the torch. If he wanted, he could reach up and touch it with his fingers. And the incline grew steadily steeper.

MINUTES LATER, ALMOST giving up hope, Molly spotted something in the ceiling illuminated by Michael's light. He kept going, but she searched for the spot with her beam. At last, she found the opening.

It was only a few inches across, nothing like the cave mouth they'd been hoping for. But the sweet scent of grass was stronger.

"Michael."

He turned, and soft light was diffused over his handsome features. "What?"

"There's a hole." Molly shone her light so he could see it.

"Missed that. You're brilliant." Michael joined her and peered up. Then he shone his flashlight around the cave, searching for something.

"What are you looking for?"

"I don't understand what that hole's doing there."

"Fresh air? To let out coal gas?"

"Can you tell how deep it is?"

"No."

After a brief search, Michael found a small collection of rocks with rotted twine bound around them. He grinned like a loon, but Molly didn't understand why.

"What have you got?"

He pocketed the stones. "In a minute." He switched his light off and put it away. "Let me give you a boost and see what you can discover here." He knelt, closed his arms around her thighs and slowly lifted her. "Watch your head, love."

Gingerly, Molly reached up for the ceiling of the tunnel and eased herself against the ragged stone. She shone the light.

"What can you see?"

"It's a hole. About six inches in diameter."

"Natural or cut?"

Molly studied the sides of the opening. "It's too uniform to be natural."

"So someone cut a hole there."

"Yes, but as I said before, that could be to prevent a coal-gas buildup."

Michael grinned at her. "Could be for something else, too."

"What?"

"How far do you think we've come?"

"From the prison cell?"

"Yes."

Molly had no idea. It seemed they'd been walking for hours. "A couple of miles, maybe."

"Make that five miles, but three of them have been more or less straight south. I'm thinking we shouldn't be far from Blackpool now."

Lydia stared at him. "How do you know that?"

Molly smiled, knowing her husband. "Because Michael is a habitual counter. Although he won't readily admit it, he has a touch of obsessive-compulsive disorder. He's been counting steps since we escaped."

"As well as taking away those where we doubled back on ourselves." Michael waggled his torch over the ceiling. "That hole, I believe, confirms our proximity to town."

"How?"

"Charles Crowe needed to go into Blackpool to check on safe sailing conditions for his slave ships. He'd find out if anyone was watching, or if British patrols or rivals were in town. Of course, he wouldn't want to sail all the way back to the slave pens, because that would take too much time."

Glancing up at the hole, Molly understood the mystery

of the knotted stones. "Crowe needed a way to signal his men."

"Couldn't his men have simply entered the tunnels under the town buildings?" Lydia looked at Michael.

Michael smiled. "There was a lot of business going on through those tunnels back then, Miss Crowe. Your ancestor wasn't the only man looking to make a dishonest living or avoid paying taxes. Maybe Charles Crowe kept himself separate from the slave crew in Blackpool." He played his light over the hole. "So he used this."

"Surely he didn't just yell orders down through the hole?" Lydia asked.

Molly shook her head. "Those stones Michael picked up? They had bits of rotted string tied around them. Your ancestor probably tied messages around the rocks and dropped them down this hole."

"Or maybe he simply used bits of colored cloth." Michael shifted to a new position. "It didn't have to be a complicated message. It just had to indicate whether or not the ship could set sail."

Lydia peered up at the ceiling. "Then where does that hole lead?"

"Somewhere outside of Blackpool maybe. Not far. He'd want to be able to get a message quickly to whomever waited in this area. If we can find this spot later when we're outside the tunnel, I'm willing to wager that there's a monument of some sort to mark the location."

Brow furrowed in thought, Lydia waited a moment, then took a breath. "Maybe a wishing well?"

"That would be perfect, but why a wishing well?"

"Because there's one on an old road my family used to take into Blackpool. Before the new highway was laid in. I rode motorbikes along it when I was a teen. There are so many things around Crowe's Nest that I never truly thought about it." Lydia shook her head. "I'm afraid my family has always been filled with secrets."

"Whether there's a wishing well at the other end of that hole or not, we know we're getting closer to Blackpool. How far is the well from the town?"

"No more than a half mile or so. Our holdings round Crowe's Nest butt up against the town."

"I didn't think it would be far from either the town or your home. Charles Crowe would have wanted to keep an eye on everything." Michael reached into his pocket and brought out the iPod. "Good. There's still some battery left."

"You're going to listen to music?" Lydia frowned.

"Not hardly. With the popularity of the iPhone, most people forget that the iPod Touch has Wi-Fi capability."

"I don't understand."

Molly did, and she leaned down and kissed Michael on the head. "If we can get a signal, we can send a message. I suppose you have someone in mind, Michael?"

He grinned. "I told Iris I was coming to get you. She's manning the phones at home. You have Wi-Fi at Crowe's Nest?"

"Of course. But it's encrypted."

"Then you'll tell us the password. Easy peasey."

Molly took the iPod Touch from Michael's hand. He was all smiles. He believed in technology a lot more than she did.

Lydia seemed doubtful, too. "But we're so far away from the house."

"How far?"

Molly shoved the iPod as far up into the hole as she could.

"Two hundred yards," Lydia said, "give or take."

"Most people don't realize how far a LAN—a local area network—will transmit. Do you have Wi-Fi throughout the manor house?"

"Of course. I can get the signal on my laptop when I'm out on the patio."

"There you go. You can bet your routers are pushing a significantly enhanced signal. Or that there are repeaters all over the house. Or a combination of both. Wi-Fi signals have actually been picked up over a mile away, under optimum conditions. All we're asking for is a couple hundred yards."

After a moment, Molly pulled the iPod back down and looked at it. She smiled broadly when she saw the readout. "It's trying to connect. It wants a password."

Michael heaved a sigh of relief. "Brill."

Lydia gave Molly the password, a confusing combination of letters, numbers and symbols that she felt she would never have been able to remember. After she keyed the last one in, she waited until she got the confirmation screen. "I'm in."

"Good. Now send Iris a message. I doubt Paddington is very tech savvy."

"Neither is Aleister." Lydia looked unhappy.

Molly typed furiously on the small keyboard.

Iris?

For a moment, the cursor simply hung there in limbo and she started to think that the connection had failed after all. Then a message came back.

Michael?

It's Molly.

Thank God. Are you and Michael all right?

We're trapped in the caves beneath Blackpool. We need help.

What can I do?

Molly gazed down at Michael. "She wants to know what we'd like her to do."

"Wake up Paddington and bring him up to speed, for starters. Now that we're away and not directly in Draghici's hands, we can risk that."

Molly relayed the message.

Where should I direct him to look for you?

Molly posed the question to Michael.

After a quiet moment, Michael shook his head. "Tell her that we don't know. It will hopefully be somewhere in Blackpool. Paddington should still just stay alert and hope to find us once we're able to be precise about our location. And he should also notify and watch over Aleister Crowe."

"Why worry about my brother?" Lydia looked confused.

"You don't want Draghici and his men to target him now that you've made your escape." Molly supplied the answer before Michael was able to arrive at one.

Michael smiled faintly. "A Crowe in hand, so to speak, is still worth ransoming."

"And Aleister's already involved," Molly said. "I'm sure Draghici has been in touch with him about your ransom." She typed the message up, then sent it. "Okay."

Gently, Michael placed her back on her feet. She handed him the iPod. "Smart thinking."

"Technology is bloody awesome, love. I've told you that before."

"I know. I've developed a new respect for it." Despite the shared moment of levity, overwhelming despair raged quietly in the back of Molly's mind, ready to pounce.

"Do we still have the connection?"

Molly checked, then shook her head.

"That would be too much to hope for."

They heard the voices in the tunnel again. Realizing that Draghici and his band had once more found them, panic burst like a bombshell inside her.

"Time to go." Michael pointed his light at the entry ahead of them and they ran.

CHAPTER TWENTY-TWO

THEY WERE LESS THAN half a mile away from Blackpool. *Stay with it,* Molly urged herself. *Just keep putting one foot in front of the other.*

The voices grew steadily louder behind them, like hounds closing in for the kill.

"They're catching up." Lydia was approaching another full-blown panic.

"We're almost home." Michael still held on to her elbow and propelled her at greater speed than she could have managed on her own. "Just keep thinking that."

The stairs at the end of the tunnel came up suddenly and Molly couldn't stop herself in time. She tried to leap onto them but slipped off one and turned her ankle painfully. Her hands broke her fall as her flashlight skidded away. Her chin banged against the steps in front of her and bright lights exploded behind her eyes. The impact knocked the wind from her lungs.

"Molly!" Michael rushed forward and tried to help her to her feet.

Managing her panic, Molly fought to suck in a breath. "I'm fine." Brushing his hands away, she stood, embarrassed at her inelegance. But in the next moment, she chided herself for feeling embarrassed given the situation they were in. She picked up the flashlight and scanned the steps.

They led up to an arched doorway someone had built a long time ago. Most of the stones were rubbed smooth by frequent passage, and two of them were missing, resembling vacant teeth.

"Can you carry on?"

"Yes." Molly shone her light inside the small room. The space was almost square, as long as it was tall. All four walls contained narrow doorways that looked just like the one she'd stepped through.

"You're bleeding, love." Tenderly, Michael pulled up his shirttail and blotted her face.

The effort stung sharply enough that Molly drew back.

"Sorry." Michael kissed her forehead. "Now, let's see what you've discovered."

"We don't have time." The sound of the approaching men grew louder in Molly's ears.

"Molly, we have to take time." He didn't look at her while he was speaking. His light moved incessantly around the walls of the room. "We've already heard about Charles Crowe's nasty little penchant for traps from the local spelunkers."

The tunnel explorers around Blackpool attributed the traps to Charles Crowe's efforts to hide his treasure, but that didn't mean they were all of Crowe's design.

Molly immediately grasped what Michael was getting at. "And there's no reason why this place would have been constructed with so much attention to detail."

Michael nodded. "Down one or more of those passageways, I'd be willing to wager that Charles Crowe left some deadly little surprises."

Excitement flared inside Molly, but it paled in comparison to the fear that writhed within her. She didn't know how much time they had before Draghici and his thugs found them. "It can only mean we're close to Charles Crowe's ultimate hiding place."

"That's insane." Lydia went to one of the passageways and peered into the darkness. "There is no treasure. If there had been, the family would have found it long ago."

"I didn't say there was a treasure." Michael studied the walls, then lifted his light to the ceiling. "I said there was a hiding place." He paused, then shifted the light and reached up to brush at the accumulated dust and lampblack. "Well, hello."

Michael's fingers trailed over the ceiling, following an engraved line he'd found there. He slipped the Leatherman multitool from his pocket and opened a Phillips screwdriver attachment. His renewed scraping produced a cloud of dust and debris that coated his face and he had to stop occasionally to wipe stray bits from his eyes.

When he finished, though, the image of a bird in full flight was revealed.

"What is that?" Michael scrubbed at his tear-streaked eyes and tried to focus.

"Definitely a bird." Molly studied the carving. "If I had to guess, I'd say it's a crow."

Michael smiled. "Narcissistic bugger, wasn't he?"

"I thought we'd already established that."

Lydia screamed.

When Molly swiveled her light back she saw that Lydia had gone through one of the doors and into the passageway.

Lydia screamed again.

The men's voices out in the tunnel quieted, and Molly

knew they must have heard Lydia's cries. The sounds of their approach redoubled.

Michael strode into the passageway with the pistol in his fist. "Lydia?"

"Here. I'm sorry. I'm sorry. I couldn't help myself."

Molly stepped in behind Michael and peered down the tunnel. Lydia leaned against one of the walls and shook as she silently cried. She had her left forearm pressed against her mouth. Tears cut tracks down the dust that coated her face.

On the floor, a skeleton knelt with an iron spear shoved through the empty space where his guts should have been. Enough remnants of clothing remained to identify him as male, or a female dressed as a man. The spear had come out from the wall and a tumble of rock blocked further passage.

Michael put the pistol in his waistband and knelt down to examine the skeleton.

Lydia peeled herself off the wall and came running to Molly, who wrapped her arms around the young woman. "Michael?"

"In a moment. If there's something here to learn, we may need to know it."

FROM THE CUT OF THE CLOTHING, Michael ruled out the dead man being from Charles Crowe's time. The clothing was at least fifty or so years later. A suit, from the looks of it. Definitely not an expensive one, but no one these days wore a suit to go spelunking in.

Sorting through the man's pockets, Michael found nothing. Whatever personal possessions he'd had on him had vanished. Probably one of Draghici's little band had found the skeleton while wandering the tunnels. Or maybe a spelunker from earlier times.

Moving the torch around, Michael spotted the skeletal hand of another victim sticking out from the tumble of rock. Charles Crowe certainly hadn't played around with his vicious death traps. Behind this second victim was a dead end.

Red eyes gleamed in the shadows of the rocks. Rats. Michael hoped the little beasts didn't choose to put in an appearance. Molly wouldn't react well to their intrusion.

Just as he started to get up, the torchlight caught something inside one of the dead man's boots. With two fingers, he carefully removed a small leather-bound journal.

"Michael."

"Coming. Just give me a moment."

"Draghici and his men know where we are. Hurry!"

Entranced, Michael opened the journal and found two pencils, a fountain pen that had long gone dry and a narrative written in ink in a precise hand.

This journal belongs to Elliott Crane of Leister, England, Intrepid Explorer and Discoverer of all Lost Secrets.

The first entry was logged *26 December, 1936*.

Dearest Glinda,
I do hope you enjoy your little gaff. All the fellows thought the idea of you giving me an "explorer's" journal quite the joke. At my expense. So it only

stands to reason that I dedicate my first entry to
you. However, I will have you know that my forays
into abandoned or neglected bits of history might
one day provide us with a means of support after
we are married. Also, since I know that you will
always avail yourself of this book anytime you've
an inclination to, I will also say—

"Michael!"

Michael closed the journal and shoved it into his
pocket. He darted back to Molly and Lydia. "Sorry."

The approaching men sounded much nearer now.

Molly shone her torch over the remaining two tunnels.
"Do you think these have traps?"

"Definitely. Charles Crowe wouldn't have wanted
anyone to find what he'd hidden."

"So we have a fifty-fifty chance of picking the right
one. Do you feel lucky?"

"Lucky?" Michael stared at the two openings and
considered how hard Crowe had worked to maintain
his secrets. The wily old pirate and slave trader hadn't
wanted anyone to know his business. He'd even dug the
communications hole to the passageway to give his men
a faster response time.

The man had been a master at planning and mis-
direction.

"Michael?"

"Give me a minute, love."

"We don't have a minute."

Still absorbed in the thread of thought he was following, Michael looked at Molly. "Think about it.
Charles Crowe was a gamesman. He liked puzzles and
challenges."

"Draghici and his men are coming."

"Take this room. Look at how it's designed. The formation isn't natural." Michael waved his torch around the room. "This is a deliberate bit of theatrics. What was the first reaction you had when you entered this room?"

Molly gazed into his eyes and he knew she was making an effort to figure out where he was going. "I thought that this was the entrance to his hiding place."

Michael smiled tightly. "Yes. And I believe that it is." He pointed at the two unexplored passageways. "I also believe both of those hold only death traps. Crowe wouldn't leave the path to his secret stash open for someone to find. He'd be much more devious about it." He tilted his head. "In a game, I'd do the same. But I'd provide clues for the player to find."

"There are no clues."

"Aren't there?" Michael took out the Leatherman multitool again and started scratching at the ceiling. "Why show the picture of a crow?"

"To make a statement."

"Sure. But also to draw attention to it." When the tool failed to uncover anything, Michael's nerves tightened. He was certain only death awaited them down the passages, but Draghici and his men wouldn't be any more generous. "This crow is *flying*."

"Up?"

"That's what I'm hoping."

Lydia stood in Molly's shadow and gazed upward. She whispered hoarsely when she spoke. "'Crows rise above.' That's the—"

"Family motto." Michael nodded and kept scraping. "I know. I've seen it."

"Charles Crowe is the one who instituted that saying," Lydia told them.

The knife blade suddenly stopped, caught on a crevice buried in the accumulated grime. Michael couldn't help grinning. Working quickly, he uncovered a circle that more than encompassed the carving of the flying bird of prey.

When he stepped back, they all knew what it was.

"A door?" Lydia gawped at the circle. "But how do you open it?"

Michael was already searching the ceiling. "Molly, take a look at the walls. There has to be a switch or—"

"Here!" Molly shone her light on a stone inset nearby. The stone was only a foot and a half from the floor and almost hidden by the stones that framed the door they'd originally come through. A small, skeletal-looking raven had been inscribed there.

Michael stepped back from the circle he'd uncovered and took Lydia with him. He wasn't willing to believe that Charles Crowe didn't have one more death trap at the ready. The man hadn't merely taken advantage of the natural formations in the cave system at this point. He'd improved upon them. "Press it."

Molly dropped to one knee and shoved with both hands. Michael was just about convinced that there was another trick or that the engraving was a false lead—or that the device might have gotten permanently stuck— when the crow carving moved with a shrill grating.

Machinery shifted above the stone ceiling. Michael felt the vibrations up his legs. Lydia threw her arms around him and clung as if for dear life.

With inexorable slowness, the circular cut slid down out of the ceiling and exposed three rusty metal rods that were bolted into the stone. The rods lowered the trap door, creating a black hole a couple inches wide into a tunnel above.

CHAPTER TWENTY-THREE

MESMERIZED, MICHAEL STARED at the apparatus. "Some kind of winch assembly lowered that. Doubtless it pulls it back up again."

"Michael." Molly pushed at him. "We've got to go."

They could hear men shouting through the door. "In there!"

"There's nowhere to go out of that room!"

Michael switched off his torch, put it in his pocket and formed a stirrup with his hands and nodded at Molly. "Up you go, love."

"Michael."

"No time to argue."

Molly stepped into his hands and he boosted her up. The light went with her. She pulled herself over the edge and through the hole, and only then did Michael realize that he might have just delivered her to her death. "Molly?"

She stuck her face back through the opening. "There's another passageway. Hurry."

Michael formed a stirrup again and lifted Lydia, as well. Molly helped guide the younger woman through. As soon as her weight was out of his hands, Michael leaped up and grabbed the lip of the opening. He hauled himself up just as the door burst open and lights flooded the room below.

Draghici yelled curses. "I know you've got a gun, Michael Graham. If you give it up, I'll let you and your missus live."

Not bloody likely. Michael stood inside the passageway and took out his torch, adding its light to Molly's.

Three passageways loomed before them, none of them natural.

Michael took a deep breath. "God, I do so hate Charles Crowe."

"Which way?" Molly scanned the walls with her torch.

"I don't know." Michael stepped forward. "I'll go—"

"To the right. It's as good a guess as any, and I won't have you taking every risk."

Before Michael could dissuade her, Molly disappeared into the passageway on the right. Lydia followed her immediately, then screamed.

Panicked, Michael peered into the narrow tunnel, expecting another skeleton. Instead, he saw only Molly, with Lydia nowhere in sight.

"She fell!" Molly's face was ghost-white.

"Michael!"

Glancing down, heart banging at the back of his throat, he saw Lydia revealed in his torchlight. She clung desperately to an outcrop of rock that hung over an abyss.

Lowering himself on one knee, Michael caught hold of her wrist and pulled her up.

As they soothed the shaking woman, Draghici's voice below drew Michael's attention.

"Did you hear me, Michael Graham? I'll not be asking again."

They returned to the opening.

"Two passages to go." Michael gave Molly his torch.

"I don't see another secret door."

"We didn't see the last one, love." Michael tracked her movements and at the same time watched for activity through the hole to the lower room.

"Or the drop-off."

"That was a nasty bit of business, and I'm sure we can only expect more of the same."

"Charles Crowe was a very sadistic man."

"Couldn't agree with you more. Shine the torch a little to your left."

Molly did, and Michael spotted a small lever jutting from the wall. There was no reason to hide the door's operations up here. He hoped it would allow them to close the entrance before Draghici and his gang discovered it. He pulled the lever and the machinery ground away again.

More rapidly than it had lowered, the trap door rose. The long rods pulled up into a metal structure bolted into the stone walls around it. Michael thought about that. "It's counterweighted, but easier going up than down. That's interesting."

"What's interesting about that?" The light darted about as Molly continued searching.

"If the mechanism failed, or was jammed somehow, no one below would be able to climb up into this area."

"So Charles Crowe and his treasure would be safe from anyone looking for it?"

"And perhaps from his crew. I'm sure they were an avaricious lot themselves. Like tends to attract like."

"That's why we're together."

Michael smiled at her through the darkness.

The door continued to rise as Draghici and his men realized what was happening and looked up. One of them caught hold of the circular plate and hauled himself up.

He can't make it, Michael thought. *There isn't time.* Stunned, he watched as the man scrambled onto the platform. Michael lifted the pistol.

The man pointed his own gun at Michael as he tried to gain his footing on the plate. Before he could draw up his legs completely, the platform closed on his thighs like the jaws of a monstrous beast. Flesh pulped and bone cracked. The gypsy screamed in agony and dropped his weapon.

Lydia gave a cry and turned away. Molly averted her face.

Even though the man meant him harm, probably would have killed him, Michael shoved his pistol into the waistband of his pants and grabbed the trapped gypsy's arm. Although he pulled as hard as he could, the man didn't budge. The stone held tight but mercifully the mechanism had stopped for the moment.

"Draghici!" Michael had to yell over the man's screams. "Draghici!"

"I hear you, Graham."

"Your man is caught. There's a release down there."

Lydia stared at Michael. "No. You can't tell them."

Michael turned on her, angry because he felt so helpless. "I can't let him die." *And I can't get us out of here.* He raised his voice. "Over by the door. Near the bottom on the right-hand side."

The trapped man went slack. At first, Michael thought

he'd just passed out from the pain, but when he put his fingers against the fellow's throat, there was no pulse. Swallowing the sudden sickness that pooled at the back of his own throat, Michael peered through the narrow gap between the platform and the floor.

Draghici was on his hands and knees at the wall, shoving the bricks with both hands. "It's not working!"

"It's too late. He's dead." Michael stared at the blood spilling into the lower room. Droplets splattered on the group below.

"Your fault, Graham. You killed him."

Ignoring the accusation, Michael turned his thoughts to survival and started going through the dead man's clothes. He took the pistol equipped with a minitorch, then took a full-size torch from the man's coat.

"Find something to pry that rock open," Draghici ordered his men below. "Do it now." The gypsy leader stood up and tried his mobile. Evidently there was no signal because he cursed and shoved it back in his pocket. Michael wondered who Draghici was calling. The ransom demand for Lydia had surely already been met by Aleister.

Michael turned to Molly. "Draghici's got men outside the caves. Probably in town." Even when they got topside, they wouldn't necessarily be safe.

Michael finished searching the man's clothes. There was a mobile under his shirt, tucked into his waistband. Michael took it, powered it on and checked the battery. It was nearly fully charged.

"A bit of luck with the mobile." A quick glance at the signal bars confirmed that he was as unfortunate as Draghici. "But no luck on a connection."

"Look out!" Lydia pointed at the gap in the floor.

One of the gypsies had climbed up and was pointing his pistol through the opening beside his companion's dead body. Michael stood, took a step and stomped on the gypsy's hand. Bones cracked and the man yelled harshly. The gun slipped free and slid through the gap as the man tumbled backward.

Two other goons thrust their hands through the hole, as well, and Michael turned back to Lydia and Molly.

They still had a decision to make and no time to make it.

"This way." Molly pointed to a carved single line on top of the entry. "I've got an idea."

Once they were inside the tunnel, Michael took Lydia by the hand. Shots rang out in the chamber behind them and bullets ricocheted from the walls. Thankfully the passageway was angled just enough to deflect the rounds.

Michael trained his torch on the tunnel ahead and tried not to think of the deadly things that could spring up and catch Molly unawares. Nearly fifty yards farther on, the passageway opened wide enough to present two more tunnels, once more side by side.

"Not again." Panic began to eat at his resolve. The cloistered feeling of being trapped underground closed in on him.

"Michael." Molly suddenly stood in front of him.

He focused on her and made himself calm.

"Are you listening?"

"Yes." His voice didn't sound like his own, and it echoed down the tunnels.

"I need you to take a breath."

Michael did. It was easier doing that with her watching him, but the terror still threatened to overwhelm him.

"You need to be thinking clearly while we do this."

He nodded.

Smiling, she put her hands on both sides of his face and held him. "During our years together, I've seen you do amazing things with that near-photographic memory of yours. I've watched you walk into a room full of strangers and leave with the names of every person in that room, even if you didn't talk to them."

He focused on her, but didn't know where she was going with this.

"If I asked you to, do you think you could sketch the six sides of that cube? The one that you and Rohan made that showed the tunnels beneath the town."

"Molly, I don't—"

She placed a hand on his mouth. "You found a way to break into this prison. I think I've found a way to break out. But I'm going to need your help." She reached into his pants pocket and took out the leather-bound journal he'd found on the dead man. "Draw the six sides of that cube, Michael. Do it now."

Curbing his frustration, Michael opened the journal and started drawing. He made the lines neat and precise. "I still don't see—"

"Patience. Trust me."

Down the tunnel came the sounds of metal grating against rock. Draghici and his gypsies must have found something to use as levers to pry open the platform or maybe they were trying to simply break the stone. Either way, they were coming soon.

He concentrated on the images he was drawing, sliding the pencil point deftly across the page.

"Put each side on its own page," Molly directed him.

Michael finished with the first side and went to a new page.

Finally, he was finished. He looked up at her. "You want to explain to me what that was about?"

"You saw the symbols Charles Crowe carved into the floor?" Molly was so calm he couldn't believe it.

Draghici's gypsies had evidently given up getting the platform to lower any farther and now worked at battering it to pieces. The blows rang and echoed through the tunnels.

"Of course I did, but what—?" Then he remembered how she'd pointed out the line over the door. "That marking let you know which tunnel to take."

"Yes. They're a numbered sequence, Michael. The sides of the cube are numbered, too."

Michael stared at the six images he'd drawn. One line, two lines, the triangle, the square, the pentagon and the hexagon. Finally, in that order, he saw the correlation that had been nagging at him. 1, 2, 3, 4, 5, 6.

"I think each of those cube faces is part of the map that leads to the treasure room." Molly tapped the first page with her finger. "This is the juncture where we are now. See how this line runs along, then dead-ends?"

"Yeah." Feeling more hopeful, Michael nodded. "Yeah, I see it now. Don't know why I didn't get it before."

"You did. You just didn't know how it worked."

Michael counted the twists and angles. "Five turns, then we should find a door marked with two lines."

"Right."

Behind them, they heard the stone break. Sections of the platform slammed against the rock floor.

Draghici roared up at his men. "Can you get through there yet?"

"It's big enough—"

"Then go after them. The rest of us will be along soon's we get the way clear."

Molly flickered her light toward the two tunnels. "You're going to have to lead us."

Elated, Michael kissed her. "Did I ever tell you how smart and beautiful you are?"

"Yes."

"Well, it can't be often enough." Michael pointed his torch toward the passage on the right and started down it.

CHAPTER TWENTY-FOUR

EVEN THOUGH SHE'D BEEN pretty certain of herself, and even more so when Michael saw things her way, Molly still had a grain of worry as she followed him down the passageway. They could have made the right choice, but that didn't mean Charles Crowe hadn't lined the way with traps. She wished that Michael would go slowly enough to be safe, but she heard the hounds baying at their heels.

"Find them!" Draghici's voice echoed through the tunnels. "Find them and kill them! We'll sell their bodies back for ransom!"

A chill threaded through Molly's spine. *Concentrate on what you're doing. Follow Michael. He knows the way.*

It seemed that was true. Michael flew through the underground tunnels. He never hesitated at intersections. His flashlight only flicked over the markings.

He's in the game. The thought brought a smile to Molly's face. She didn't know how many times she'd walked in on him to see him totally enraptured by a game he was designing or playing. In the early days of their relationship, she'd admit to sometimes being jealous. But only a little. Games took Michael away from her, but they enriched and invigorated him as nothing else did. Not even her. She knew he would never want to be in a position to choose between her and the games. She would never put him there.

Charles Crowe and his underground labyrinth had met their match in Michael.

Lydia looked back at her. The young woman's face was pallid in the darkness. "Does he know where he's going?"

"Definitely. You just try to keep up with him."

Draghici's men shouted behind them. Someone had found one of Charles Crowe's surprises. Screams echoed through the tunnel, followed by curses then a single gun report.

Putting someone out of his misery? Or the reflexive pull of a dying man? Molly shuddered. Either way, she didn't want to know.

A moment later, Michael paused in a new chamber and shone his light over the three man-made tunnels ahead of him. The two on the right bore markings, a square and a flying crow.

"The crow." Lydia pointed at the bird. "That's the way, right?"

Michael shook his head. "No. You'll probably discover something particularly nasty at the end of that, I'd wager. Crowe is just baiting anyone who made it this far." He pointed to the tunnel on the left and shone his light at the markings above it: two lines. "That's where we go. That's the second part of the map." He plunged through the entranceway.

Lydia followed, but her stumbling gait showed that her strength was flagging.

"You can do it, Lydia." Molly raised her voice. "Michael!"

He stopped instantly and turned back to them, careful to keep his light from hitting them in the eyes. "What?"

"A slower pace."

Chagrined, he nodded. "Sorry. Let's get down to the next turn, make sure we're not followed, then we'll take a breath."

MICHAEL MOVED HIS TORCH'S BEAM around, seeking any of Charles Crowe's lethal surprises. Grudgingly, he had to admit that he halfway admired the man. Crowe had built a deadly playground that ran for miles. He'd worked for months or years to perfect the map.

Doubtless, some legs of the underground path were on different levels beneath the rock strata, and nearly all of the tunnels and passageways had been created by nature. Charles Crowe must have spent considerable time exploring them. More probably, he had assembled knowledge of other pirates and smugglers and put together an overview of the existing passages.

But several of the walls showed tool marks where people had dug at the tunnels. And why not? Michael thought sourly of the slaves Charles Crowe had brought into Blackpool, only to parcel them off later to the United States. Crowe wouldn't have allowed a labor pool like that to sit idle. Those slaves had quarried rock to make tunnels, and in turn that rock had been sold to build buildings in Blackpool. The horror had fed on itself.

The third leg was marked by the triangle. They jogged down to the first turn, then took a water break. Lydia looked sick and done in. Molly was nearly spent, too.

"Only a little farther." Michael drank water sparingly. Sweat and grime coated him.

"Know that for a fact?" Molly smiled at him.

"Not really. Hoping, actually."

Draghici's men sounded farther away now. Evidently they were struggling through the maze, trying to find their way.

"The good thing is that Draghici and his blokes are having a rougher go of it than we are." Michael stretched and felt the aches filling his body. "Are we ready?"

Slowly, Lydia nodded.

"Off we go, then." Michael swung back into the lead.

THEY PASSED THE SQUARE GATE. Then the pentagon. Michael remembered the twists and turns effortlessly. He was into it now, and the gamer inside him was in his element.

The batteries in his torch failed unexpectedly. He got replacements from the rucksack and installed them. The light was now so bright that it hurt his eyes at first.

Molly's torch had turned orange.

"Let's replace those batteries, as well." Michael handed her his.

"Shouldn't we wait until they completely go out?"

"We've got spares. And we're halfway through the fifth section of the map. If Charles Crowe left any cute ways of killing explorers, we'll soon find them." He knew he'd said too much when she blanched. "Sorry."

"No. I need to keep that in mind. We both do."

Michael replaced the batteries and returned the torch to her. The one she'd been carrying was lighter.

"You, too."

"I am." Michael turned back to the darkness.

THE LAST TUNNEL ENDED and another one started. The new one had a gate with a hexagon carved over it.

"Is this it?" Molly directed her beam in one direction, while Michael shone his in the other. She started to walk toward the entrance.

"Molly, don't walk any—"

The floor shifted beneath Molly, but even that small instance of warning wasn't enough to prepare her for the ground dropping under her. She tried to scream, but the sound caught in her throat and wouldn't budge.

She fell.

Something hot, hard and unrelenting closed around her left wrist as she flung her arms out to grab on to something—anything—to stop her fall. Abruptly, she swung into the rocky side of the pit. She let her flashlight hang from the strap as she clawed at the rock and kicked her feet, trying to find purchase with her boots.

She gazed up and saw Michael holding on to her, one hand closed tight around her wrist.

"Not time to go yet, love."

Silently, struggling to stay calm, Molly made herself stop clawing at the rocky wall and clasp her hand on top of Michael's wrist. "Oh, God, Michael." Her voice was a hoarse whisper.

"Just hold on. I'll have you out of there in a jiff." Michael gripped her other wrist with his free hand.

Lydia moved in behind him and picked up the flashlight. She shone it down over both of them.

"Don't shine it in her eyes." Michael shifted his hold.

"Sorry."

"It's all right. Just keep the light to the side."

Lydia redirected the beam.

Michael started pulling slowly. "The trick now is to not pull your arms out of their sockets."

"If it will get me back on solid ground, I don't care."

"You'll care tomorrow."

"As long as there is a tomorrow."

"Brace your feet and lean out a little so you can get a grip with your boots. I'm in an awkward position here. Can't get the leverage I need."

Molly tried not to think about how deep the pit was, but the thought was there anyway.

"Keep breathing, love. Can't have you passing out."

Making herself take a breath, Molly leaned back and pushed up with her legs. Gradually, inch by inch, she fought her way back to level ground—*solid* ground—with Michael's help. When she was safe, they sat there for a moment, silent. Then they laughed, and Molly knew it was because they were still alive, still together. That relief and love was so great that it couldn't be contained. It had to come out somehow.

"God." Lydia slumped to the ground a couple of feet away. The light shook on the wall from her trembling. "The two of you are loons. Truly you are. How many times did you have to go through things like this before you got used to it?"

"Counting this one?" Michael got to his feet and helped Molly to hers.

Lydia just stared at him.

"One."

"You're both daft."

Michael smiled. "Not so daft that we'd ever want to go through it again."

But you would, wouldn't you? Staring at her husband,

Molly knew the answer. All the mysteries they'd solved in Blackpool thus far had revealed a lot about themselves that they hadn't known before. Before moving to the town, they'd never gotten to play detective. Never hunted murderers. Never gotten in harm's way outside of a rocky plane flight or a fender bender.

She recalled the light in her uncle Peter's eyes when he'd talked about a particularly vicious or dangerous piece of work he'd done with the Mystery Casefiles Agency. He was addicted to the investigations. She'd always just thought he liked telling stories, but now she had a better understanding.

Michael focused on her. "Maybe we could show a little restraint. In this part of the game, you have to think and be quick at the same time in order to seize the prize. Going haring about isn't a good idea."

"I wasn't 'haring about.' I was just having a look around."

"Impatience will kill you, love."

Exasperated, Lydia stood. "So will sitting here. Draghici and his people may not seem to be on top of us at the moment, but they're out there."

"I know." Michael plucked his flashlight from her grip. "We need to find a hexagon in the worst way."

Molly shone her light at the ceiling, thinking maybe there was another way out. "Do you know where we are, Michael? Have you been able to keep track?"

"My best guess is that we're not back in Blackpool."

That disappointed her almost as much as not finding the hexagon carved into the ceiling. "Then where?"

"If I've figured everything right, we should be somewhere near Crowe's Nest."

"That can't be possible." Lydia felt along the wall without the aid of a flashlight.

"Until tonight, I daresay you would have thought this underground labyrinth was an impossibility."

She didn't argue.

Frustrated, Molly took a breath that made her bruised back and ribs ache fiercely. *Think bigger.* Michael was looking for the answer in the small details. If Charles Crowe truly wanted to hide a door—

Then she saw it. "Michael."

Even though her call came out as a whisper, he heard her and turned. "Yes?"

"You're searching for a hexagon, but you're thinking too small." Slowly, Molly traced the outlines of the hexagon formed by the stones on the wall they'd faced after stepping out of the tunnel.

"The whole wall?" Michael stared at the outline in disbelief. Then he walked over to it. "There are smaller stones at every angle formed by the hexagon." He pushed one of them and it gave a reluctant click.

Molly tried to push another one into a locked position, but she wasn't strong enough. She stepped back as Michael worked his way around the hexagon.

When he finished the last stone, down on his knees, the trap sprung.

CHAPTER TWENTY-FIVE

"LOOK OUT!" MOLLY DARTED forward, but she was already too late.

The heavy hexagonal door revolved, flipping top over bottom, propelling its massive weight toward Michael. Unbelievably quick, he dived under the massive door and into the space beyond.

"Michael!" Molly raced to the door and pushed, thinking that the locks would have reset and she'd have to initiate the sequence again. Instead, the door swung inward once more and stopped. "Michael!"

"I'm fine." Michael stood in a small room and shone his flashlight around. "That door was an unpleasant surprise."

"You're lucky you didn't get brained." Molly climbed around the door and Lydia followed.

"I was thinking the same thing." Michael turned his attention back to the door and smiled. "Weighted door. Nifty. I'll have to remember that one. I haven't used a weighted door before. Should be easy to emulate in a game." He stepped to the wall and flicked door latches into place. "This will reset the combination locks. I don't think Draghici and his men will make it this far, but in case they do, we'll let them figure out the way in by themselves."

"Probably be a lot easier now that the hexagon will show up so well after spinning."

"True, but if they're standing too close, they might find themselves knocked out cold."

"Too bad I spoiled the other trap."

"I'll forgive you this time." Michael motioned with the flashlight. "Let's go. Shouldn't be much farther now. And if I'm right about our location, Lydia, you should practically be home. But we'll need to be careful. Obviously Charles Crowe's little surprises turn more nasty the closer we get to his roost."

AFTER THE FINAL CLIMB UP a flight of narrow stairs carved from the natural rock, Michael made out a heavy stone door ahead of him. A flying crow cut into the stone peered down at them over its cruel beak.

Molly added her torchlight to his. "Do you think there are any more traps?"

"Only one way to know, love." Michael strode forward and searched the door. He found four catches and released them, then hooked his fingers in a recessed area and pulled.

He stared in amazement into the small room that had gold bars stacked on the remnants of wooden timbers. Gold urns held gems and jewelry. He recognized a few statues from Nanny Myrie's pictures. He had no idea of the monetary value of what they were looking at, but it was definitely a fortune.

"The stories were all true," Lydia whispered. "The gypsy gold. All of it." Slowly, in stunned fascination, she walked toward the gold bars and gems.

"Have a care now." Michael gently took her wrist. "You don't know what surprises may still be lurking in this room." But he found himself moving with her, the little boy inside him awakening at their discovery. He felt like Uncle Scrooge playing in his vault.

Then he realized where this money had come from—stealing from the gypsies, selling other people into suffering and hardship and poverty till the day they died. He wanted nothing to do with any of it.

He turned the torch away just as Lydia scooped her hand through an urn filled with gems. She squealed a little.

Molly stood at the entrance and made no move toward the wealth. Michael would have bet everything he'd ever made that she was thinking the same thing he was.

He shone his torch around the room. "Let's see if we can find a way out of here. If we are around Crowe's Nest, it should be a simple matter to give Paddington a call and start setting things to rights."

"Michael."

Molly picked up a thick, dusty book from a pedestal in the corner of the room.

"What's that?"

She opened the cover and leafed through the pages. "It's a log. Charles Crowe's." She turned more pages. "It's a recording of every slave ship that sailed under his orders. And it lists names." She looked at him. "Some of these people, Michael? They're *big* names. Houses of Lords big. If I can recognize them as an American, everyone in England will know them."

"Well, if that book falls into the wrong hands, it's going to cause quite a stink." A memory twigged in Michael's brain of someone saying something very similar. "You know, love, our lives in Blackpool got more complicated when a certain solicitor showed up."

"You mean Lockwood Nightingale?"

"Exactly."

"He'd be just the man the people named in that log would send to ensure none of their ancestors' dirt touched their coattails." Molly closed the book. "I think we should have a talk with Inspector Paddington."

Michael took off the rucksack and unzipped it. "Why don't we take that along with us?"

"You can't do that." Lydia had been watching them all along. Now she stepped forward. "That book belongs to my family."

Molly turned on her, fire in her voice. "This fortune, and a considerable number of fortunes outside the room, were financed on human misery, Lydia. Do you really want to cover it up?"

Lydia hesitated.

"Maybe it's too late to do anything about those people that are dead and gone," Molly continued, "but Crowe's descendants—your brother included—might be shamed into doing something honorable with their fortunes. Reparations can be made. There are nations in West Africa that could use financial help. Draghici and his lot don't deserve the money, but other gypsy clans might be entitled to it."

Chastened, Lydia stood quietly.

"At the very least, it's something to think about." Molly handed the log to Michael, who placed it in the rucksack.

"Aleister won't like it."

"Probably not, but he'll only be the first among many." Molly directed her torch toward the shelves that occupied one wall behind stacks of gold. "Look at this."

Michael joined her. His torchlight fell over a collection

of tribal jewelry and artifacts—skulls and gems, carved ivory and beaten copper. All of it held the stories of past cultures, some of which had disappeared in the passage of years.

He took a deep breath and let it out. "This is what Rohan was searching for. This is why he came to Blackpool." He paused. "I wish he were here now."

"He'll see it soon enough." Molly raised her voice so Lydia could hear her clearly. "This definitely can't be kept secret, Lydia. All of it belongs to the people it was taken from. This is their history, their past."

"I get it, okay? Can we please go? I'm tired of being down here. It feels like I'm standing in a grave."

MICHAEL SEARCHED THE ROOM until he found a lever. When he pulled it, and the now familiar sound of machinery clanked to life. As he watched, a section of the ceiling shifted and came loose, descending on rusty iron rods. This platform was rectangular and shaped just like a—

"That's a coffin!" Molly shone her torch on the metal-and-wood box that rested on the platform.

Lydia drew back with a cry of alarm. "Oh, my God. I know where we are. We're in the family mausoleum on the estate."

Totally amazed, Michael stared at the coffin. The woods were rich, perhaps mahogany, and carried a red luster beneath the thick coats of lacquer. Gold trim edged the box.

"You *are* standing in a grave, Lydia." Michael played his torch over the top of the casket. A gold plate was screwed into place, and the name was inscribed with skill and verve.

CHARLES CROWE
1769–1841
MAY HE ETERNALLY REST

Michael had to laugh.

"What's so funny?" Molly looked at him with concern.

"C'mon, love. Don't you see the irony in this? Chuck here screwed everybody over by dying peacefully. But he arranged it so that he took his fortune with him. You don't see many people who get the chance to do that."

"But he didn't die peacefully." Lydia spoke quietly and her gaze never left the coffin. "He was murdered."

"Murdered?" The announcement sobered Michael immediately. "Everything I've read said Charles Crowe's death was the result of natural causes."

"All lies. That's what Charles Crowe's son decided to tell everyone." Lydia nodded toward the coffin. "If you open that box and have a peek inside, you'll find that someone shot Charles Crowe in the back of the head. It was done at close range."

"Someone he trusted?"

"Charles Crowe didn't seem like the trusting sort," Lydia said.

Michael silently agreed.

"There was talk of a woman assassin." Lydia shrugged. "Aleister told my brother and me all the old stories when we were children. Aleister believed them, but none of the rest of us cared. We didn't know the man, and everything we heard of him suggested that he was someone we would count our blessings never to meet."

"He definitely had a knack for making enemies of all the wrong people."

Lydia swallowed with effort. "Charles Crowe was the Bogeyman our parents would sometimes threaten us with. They'd tell us that he wasn't really in his coffin, that he was out walking the grounds and protecting his fortune. If we behaved badly, they said they'd leave us here—in the family mausoleum—for him to find us."

"Lovely childhood." Molly shook her head.

"It wasn't all bad. I don't mean to give you that impression."

"Too late."

"The Crowe family, including my parents, have all been a little strange. My great-aunt is one of the worst."

Michael wouldn't argue about that. He drew in a breath. There, mixed in with the moldering scent of the mausoleum, was the rich aroma of fresh-mown grass. Natural light filtered into the darkness above. He waved the torch's beam toward the opening. "Why don't we get out of here? There'll be plenty of time to discuss this later."

"All right." Lydia walked toward the coffin, then hesitated.

Michael was certain that the younger woman was afraid that Charles Crowe was going to throw back the cover of his coffin and grab her. "It's all right, Lydia. He's gone. Been gone a long time."

"I know." She stiffened her resolve.

An iron ladder they hadn't noticed before in the blackness of the room was bolted to the wall and led up out of the hidden vault. Lydia went up and Molly followed. After a last look around, Michael climbed after them.

MOLLY SHONE HER FLASHLIGHT around the crypt. The small room had been dedicated to Charles Crowe. Heavy stone benches filled the space, and a pulpit stood in one corner. Latticework windows occupied three of the four walls, leaving the fourth one solid. On that wall, a black-and-white portrait of the man in his later years hung over the open rectangle where the coffin had been. Beneath the picture stood a tall stone angel with wings spread.

In the painting, Charles Crowe was an old man with tufts of white hair, sunken cheeks and a cold demeanor. He wasn't smiling. Instead, he looked as if he'd just bitten into a lemon. His suit hung on him, indicating that he'd lost weight and hadn't cared enough about his appearance to have it tailored even for the portrait sitting. He held a black cane across his knees and twin mastiffs sat on either side of him.

"Makes you wonder, doesn't it, love?" Michael clambered up out of the hidden room. "Who would kill an old man like that?"

"Who knows?" Molly agreed.

"The answer is obvious." Lydia stared at the portrait of her ancestor. "Someone who hated him very much."

"Or feared him." Molly kept her voice gentle.

"Fear is just a weaker form of hate. Helpless until it has a moment to strike, and only when everything else is spent and there's nothing left to lose."

"Is that a quote?" Michael looked impressed.

"I doubt it, but I'm studying literature in university." Lydia smiled ruefully. "Some of it is bound to rub off."

Michael led the way out of the crypt and into the mausoleum proper. The building was dark but thankfully uncluttered. Once she'd learned they were in the vault, Molly had had visions of coffins scattered everywhere, and all manner of dead Crowes ready to rise up like some kind of ravening zombie horde. *You've been paying attention to far too many of Michael's games,* she chided herself.

But before they reached the door, a shadowy figure strode through. Michael pinned the figure with his flashlight. Pistol leveled before him, Aleister Crowe stood there in a wide-legged stance, his long coat billowing softly around him. He carried the walking stick with the silver crow handle in his free hand.

"What are you doing here, Michael?" If Crowe was surprised to see his kidnapped sister, he didn't show it. The man was entirely too cold-blooded for Michael's taste.

"Returning your sister to you. Finding the treasure your family lost when Charles Crowe was murdered."

Crowe glowered at his sister. "You've been talking too much, Lydia."

"Talking too much?" Unafraid, Lydia walked toward her brother. "Aleister, I was *kidnapped.* Those men were going to kill me. They were going to kill Molly."

"The ransom's been paid. You would have been set free." Crowe's pistol never wavered from Michael's chest. "And then I would have shot Stefan Draghici."

"They weren't going to release me, Aleister. They let me see their faces. They were going to kill me and Molly."

Something flickered in Crowe's dark eyes. "I didn't know they'd taken you, too, Mrs. Graham."

"There's a lot you don't know." Michael slowly pointed back at the open rectangular pit. "Your family fortune. All you have to do is crawl in the grave with Charles Crowe. Given who you are, I wouldn't guess that would be too off-putting."

Molly kept her voice soft and low so that only Michael could hear. "Michael. Not helping."

Crowe's face hardened and Molly grew frustrated. "Why are you still pointing that gun at Michael? We've got a common enemy. Draghici."

"That's what you say. I came out here because someone has broken into the estate. They're headed this way. Brought here by you, I presume."

Michael shook his head. "They didn't follow us. We've been in the tunnels for hours. Draghici and his men are still lost somewhere in that underground labyrinth, so it can't be them…."

"It's true, Aleister." Lydia's voice sounded pleading.

"Then who are they and what are they doing here?"

The shrill ring of a mobile bounced off the crypt walls. Stunned, Michael reached into his pocket and took out the device he'd gotten from the man who'd been smashed by the crow door. The mobile rang again while he was holding it.

"Aren't you going to answer that?" Crowe stepped closer.

"Not my mobile. I pulled it off a dead man." Michael pressed the call button and held it to his ear. "Hello?"

Standing next to him, Molly heard the coarse voice at the other end. "Mr. Graham, I've been looking for you. You're a hard man to catch. Now, it appears, I've found you."

"Who is this?"

The click severing the connection echoed in the room. Only a moment later, Lockwood Nightingale entered the mausoleum from the end opposite the one Crowe had walked through. Two large men with guns trailed him.

Michael recognized one of them as Leland Darrow from the pictures he'd seen of the man.

"Ah, Aleister, I'd truly hoped you wouldn't be here when I arrived." Nightingale looked irritated. "This really is a bit of a sticky wicket we've gotten ourselves involved in."

CHAPTER TWENTY-SIX

"LOCKWOOD?" CONFUSION SHOWED for just a moment on Aleister Crowe's face, but it immediately cleared, and Molly knew that he was quickly catching up to what was going on. "What are you doing here?"

Nightingale clasped his hands behind his back. "Clearing up the mess left by your ancestor, I'm afraid."

"Draghici works for you."

"No, but Mr. Darrow did manage to convince one of Stefan's vagabonds to leak information to us. I'm not happy with his performance at this juncture, but we were fortunate that you got a hold of the mobile Mr. Darrow gave to him so he could stay in touch with us. There will be reprisals." Nightingale nodded toward the phone in Michael's hand. "We were tracking a GPS on the mobile. We'd discovered it was here, somewhere at Crowe's Nest, but we didn't know exactly where. So I decided to give it a ring." He smiled coldly. "And here you are."

"What do you want?"

Sighing theatrically, Nightingale looked put out. "Must we really go through this?" He stamped his foot impatiently. "The game is over, Aleister, and you have lost. I was hired by people who will be implicated in the scandal Graham started. They're royally upset that you didn't handle this matter yourself."

Michael turned to face Nightingale and his two

coconspirators, keeping his hands at his sides. His shirt covered the pistol tucked into his waistband. "You were sent here by at least some of those people to watch the situation."

"True. With all the problems Aleister and Blackpool have had of late, my clients were concerned that their ancestors' little financial indiscretions were going to come back to haunt them. After Mr. Graham's friend started poking his nose into things, they wanted me to take care of it." Nightingale brought his hands forward and turned them palms-up. "So here I am."

"Not exactly for the visit you claimed, then, is it?" Crowe seemed unnaturally calm in the face of everything. That made Molly even more afraid.

"Not even close. I hired Mr. Darrow and his group to help me clean up the rubbish. Including that idiot Graham nearly ran down at the hospital." Nightingale flexed his fingers inside his gloves. "Surrender your pistol, Aleister. Let's make this as painless as possible."

Crowe smirked, and Molly thought the expression made the man look more devilish than ever. Aleister Crowe was a cruel man and could be cold, but in a lot of ways, he was like Michael. Both of them were gamesmen; they just pursued different theaters of operation. "Why don't you have your men put down their weapons, Lockwood?"

"Because that's not going to happen."

"I figured as much, but I thought I'd give you the courtesy." Without hesitation, Crowe fired. The muzzle flash leaped out at least a foot from his weapon.

On the other side of the room, Lockwood Nightingale fell backward. In almost the same instant, Crowe shifted his aim and fired three more rapid shots at Darrow. He staggered back and returned fire, but the bullets went into the ceiling. Chunks of broken rock tumbled down.

Molly ducked behind one of the benches. Only a few steps over, Michael grabbed Lydia and yanked her from harm's way as bullets thudded into the portrait of Charles Crowe, ripping the canvas and chipping the wall. Michael took cover behind the stone podium.

The thunder battered Molly's skull. She gritted her teeth and tried to manage the fear that vibrated through her. Bullets chopped into the stone bench and chiseled out chips that flew in all directions.

Incredibly, Crowe was still on his feet. Darrow was down, but the other man was still firing while running toward the shelter of a bench. Crowe's gun clicked and Molly guessed it had fired dry. He whirled, his long coat flying, and dropped to one knee behind the stone bench parallel with the one where Molly hid.

Crowe replaced the magazine in his weapon and glanced at her, his dark hair falling down across his face. "Are you all right?"

"Yes."

"Stay down. This will be over in a moment." Crowe twisted and pointed his gun around the corner of the bench. He aimed and let the bullets fly.

A few feet away, Michael reached into the backpack and took out the flare gun. He had one of his two captured pistols in his other hand. He shot Molly a glance as he laid the pistol on the ground. He took the mobile from his pocket and sent it skidding across the stone floor to her.

Reaching out, Molly pinned the mobile to the floor with her palm.

"Call Paddington as soon as we're outside." Michael

picked up the pistol again. He held the flare gun in his other hand and exchanged a look with Aleister. The other man smiled. To Molly, Michael said, "Cover your eyes, then get ready to run through the window."

She nodded and rolled up till she squatted on the balls of her feet. Her thumb pressed the buttons for the Blackpool police department and hovered over Send.

Michael leaned out around the podium and pointed the flare gun at the other end of the room. He squeezed the trigger and the flare took flight. The humming scream ripped loose above the sharp punctuations of the barking pistols.

The flare struck the wall just below the ceiling and exploded into a wreath of red fire. Michael had his eyes tightly closed, but the bright illumination seeped through anyway. A heartbeat later, certain that Nightingale's bullyboy must have been blinded, he opened his eyes and lifted the pistol.

Taking quick aim, he pointed at the window behind Molly and fired. Michael's rounds cored through the window, shattering the latticework and smashing the stained-glass panes. He didn't stop firing till the pistol cycled dry, then he threw it down and grabbed Lydia's wrist.

Curbing his fear, he pushed himself to his feet and dragged the young woman after him. "Let's go!" But he was talking to Molly. Lydia had no choice but to follow him like the tail on a kite.

They covered the short distance to the window. The frame struck Michael at midthigh. He lifted his boot and broke out the remnants, clearing the way. Then he half-lifted Lydia through the window.

"Head to the main house!"

Lydia stumbled and nearly fell, then she got her feet under her and ran toward the big house in the distance. In seconds, she'd disappeared into one of the outlying gardens.

Molly leaped through the window and turned back to Michael. "C'mon."

Reaching into the bag, Michael took out one of the spare flares, popped open the Very pistol's breech and fed the fat cartridge in. The one man who hadn't been shot was starting to regain his bearings. Michael aimed the flare at him and fired.

The flare detonated and filled the open space with hellish red fire again. None of it would hurt anyone, not truly, but it would give them time to escape—including Aleister, whom he couldn't see. He fled after Molly, already feeding another cartridge into the pistol.

Outside the mausoleum, the landscape was dotted with trees, flowerbeds, topiaries and statuary. Michael had been there only once before and was glad that the estate had a number of hiding places.

Molly dropped behind a sundial nearly as big as a compact car. She had the mobile pressed to the side of her head and was talking rapidly.

Michael slid into cover beside her, then reached into the rucksack and brought out the other pistol he'd picked up from the crushed gypsy. This one had the minitorch and it flashed on when he touched the trigger. He shifted his finger from the trigger immediately. Anybody still after them would use it to track him down.

"Paddington's on his way." Molly watched the mausoleum.

"How far is he?"

"He said only minutes."

Michael shook his head. "That's too long. We could be dead by then. Or Nightingale and his people could be gone."

Harsh cracks continued blasting inside the mausoleum.

"Sounds like Aleister is still holding his own."

Molly nodded. "I think he was covering us."

"Lydia, maybe." Michael wasn't gracious enough to believe that Crowe would care what happened to them. Well, maybe Molly. "How many guns does he have?"

"I only saw the one, but he carried at least one spare reload."

"He has to have more than that or else he'd be out of bullets by now."

Flashes illuminated the darkness inside the mausoleum.

"Michael, Nightingale and Darrow must have rallied and pinned him down."

"Or vice versa."

"Either way, if he tries to withdraw from the conflict, Nightingale's men are going to shoot him. Aleister will never get away."

"I know." Michael's mind raced. "Nightingale and his men didn't get here on foot." He scanned the landscape and saw a driving path leading down to the burial chamber on the other side. He looked at Molly. "If I ask you to stay here—"

"I won't."

"Then we'll go together." Michael pointed. "Through those trees, past the topiaries there and around the building. If Nightingale has vehicles there, let's see if any of them have keys." He got up and bolted, Molly at his side.

MOLLY RAN FLAT OUT, but she knew Michael was holding back so she could keep up. She realized that she was actually endangering him by coming along, but it was too late now. And she wasn't certain that he would have left her alone. She pushed herself harder, but the ground underfoot was tricky and she was so tired from the underground trek.

She rounded a crow topiary, then a ship, and vaulted a low stone wall to cut through a flower garden filled with frog ponds and sweet-smelling fruit trees. At the other side of the garden, she placed her hands on the low wall and vaulted over. Michael cleared it in a single jump.

On the other side of a copse of trees and a bird fountain, she spotted two Land Rover SUVs parked in the private lot next to the mausoleum. She headed toward them, hoping more of Nightingale's men weren't lurking about.

Instinctively, she headed for the left side of the first Land Rover.

"Other side, love. You're not in America anymore."

Molly shifted directions and tried the door, finding it open. On the other side, Michael reached for the door release.

Seated behind the steering wheel of the second Land Rover, a man raised a pistol through his open door window. Moonlight kissed the burnished steel and Molly's breath locked in her throat for just a moment. Then she yelled.

"Behind you! The car!"

GALVANIZED BY THE FEAR in Molly's voice and his own instinct for survival, Michael came round. He didn't think anything except he didn't want to die. His hand came up and he fired.

The flare sped from the pistol and smacked into the big man behind the steering wheel. The impact of the flare knocked the man backward, but he quickly started to recover. At the same time, the flare whistled around inside the Land Rover and detonated, filling the vehicle with a bright red fireball.

Michael threw the flare gun down and sprinted across the distance separating him from the man. He couldn't allow the thug to fire his gun and possibly hurt Molly. That was his first and only thought.

Disoriented, blinded by the light, the man didn't see Michael till he was almost beside him. He tried to bring his pistol up, but Michael grabbed his wrist in both hands through the open window, twisted hard and shoved the arm back against the frame of the car. Bone snapped with a gut-churning crack. The man moaned and dropped the pistol.

Reaching through the window frame, Michael grabbed the man by the hair and smashed his face against the steering wheel. He repeated the move again and again, gripped by the adrenaline that surged through him. It wasn't until he realized that the man was limp and unconscious that he could release his hold. His breath tore through his throat.

Still angry and afraid, Michael pointed the pistol he held at the Land Rover and fired rounds into both the tires on his side of the vehicle. The big SUV sagged immediately and he knew it wasn't going anywhere.

"Michael!"

He turned and ran back toward Molly and the other Land Rover. He didn't know how many bullets he had left in the pistol, but the action hadn't blown back empty yet. That was promising.

He slid into the passenger seat and barely got the door shut before Molly pressed hard on the accelerator. He reached for the seat belt as she roared around the mausoleum.

"Do you know what you're doing?"

Molly focused on her driving, her hair blowing wildly around her. "Does it look like I know what I'm doing?"

"No."

"Then let's just see what develops."

Michael strapped himself in.

THE LAND ROVER BUCKED and swayed as it shot across the grounds. Molly switched on the headlights. She glanced at the building as she swung wide of it and cut the wheel sharply to come back toward it.

"Are we going to—"

Molly cut Michael off before he could finish his question. He sounded positively frightened. If she gave herself time to think, she was certain she'd be feeling the same way.

But there was only one way to help Aleister Crowe quickly.

She caught a brief glimpse of Crowe through the window, then she steered for the end of the building where Nightingale and his men had entered.

"Will the air bags—"

"God, I hope so." The rest of whatever Michael might have said was lost in the crash.

Molly had only brief impressions of the destruction that rained down around the Land Rover. Chunks of rock and old mortar hammered the SUV and knocked out the windshield. The air bag deployed from the steering wheel and socked Molly in the face, splitting her lips. She held on to enough of her senses to slam on the brakes and hoped that she hadn't inadvertently killed someone, yet knowing that under the circumstances she could live with it if she had.

Turning her head, she glanced at her husband. "Michael. *Michael?*" Panicked, she reached for him, noticing the cuts on his forehead and face.

Before she touched him, he sat up and pointed the pistol through the windshield. Nothing in front of them moved. He reached into a pocket and pulled out the Leatherman multitool. After he flicked out a blade with his thumb, he pierced the air bags and they deflated.

Two men staggered up from the debris. With the gray stone dust covering them, they looked like ghosts.

"Easy there." Michael shoved the pistol through the window so they could see the weapon. "You're still alive so far."

Focused on them, Molly didn't realize anyone was behind her till hot metal seared her neck.

"A gallant effort, Mrs. Graham, but one destined to failure nonetheless."

No!

"MR. GRAHAM, YOU SHOULD DROP that weapon now or I'm going to blow your pretty little wife's head from her shoulders."

Icy fear ran across Michael's shoulders and down his back when he heard Lockwood Nightingale's smarmy voice. Still holding the pistol, Michael turned to Molly.

Nightingale had dragged her out of the car and stood behind her, almost hidden by her body. He held a pistol against her jaw. "Let go this instant or I'll make you a widower."

"Michael." Molly spoke calmly. "Don't you do a thing this animal tells you to. He's going to kill us anyway."

A sickening grin spread across Nightingale's face. "You two forget who you're dealing with, the kind of power that I represent. The people I work with can make all of this go away like it never happened."

Behind Nightingale, a shadow drew up from the rubble. The long coat identified Aleister Crowe immediately, and the walking stick in his hand confirmed it. He pointed the pistol at Nightingale's back, then shoved it into his pocket. Holding the walking stick in both hands, he twisted it and pulled it apart, revealing a shining blade.

Michael was sure Molly wasn't going to sit calmly by and be murdered. The firm line of her jaw announced that to anyone who knew her. Before Nightingale realized what was going on, she turned her head into his arm and sank her teeth into his wrist, biting hard and deep.

Lunging across the console, Michael caught hold of Nightingale's pistol, yanking it away from Molly just before it went off. He held on to the hot barrel and the man's hand desperately. The slide cut his fingers, but he stopped it before it could finish chambering the next round.

Then Aleister Crowe rose up like some grim, gray wraith and plunged the sword through Nightingale's back. A shocked look twisted the solicitor's face and he tried to turn away, tried to fire his pistol one more time, but the life left him and he sank bonelessly to the ground.

Darrow—clutching a bloody arm—and the other man ran for the vehicle they thought would be waiting there. Police sirens rent the air.

Crowe put his foot against Nightingale's back and yanked his sword free. He spat on the corpse at his feet.

Michael slumped in his seat as Molly burst through the door and hugged him. Michael looked at Crowe. "Get in. When those men discover that they don't have getaway vehicles waiting out there, they may return for this one."

Without a word, blood streaming from at least two wounds in his upper body, Crowe yanked the rear passenger door open and slid inside.

The front of the SUV was crumpled, but the engine was still running. Molly backed the wrecked Land Rover from the debris of the mausoleum wall and roared up the access road. Paddington's cruiser met them before they made it halfway.

As the uniformed policemen opened their doors and ordered them out, Michael tossed the gun away and stepped out of the SUV with his hands raised over his head.

Paddington waved his men to stand down and walked up to Crowe. "Mr. Crowe, maybe you can tell me what's going on here?"

"There are men back there who tried to kill us. You'll find Leland Darrow among them. I believe you know who he is."

Paddington glanced at Molly.

"There are also several members of Stefan Draghici's

clan who tried to ransom me and Lydia." Molly shrugged. "You can go pick up what's left of them."

"Bloody lovely." Paddington eyed Molly, then Michael. He snorted in disgust. "This used to be a quiet little town before the two of you showed up."

Michael didn't say anything. He just wrapped his arms around Molly and held her close.

EPILOGUE

ON THE TELEVISION, Detective Chief Inspector Paddington addressed a group of journalists in front of the Blackpool police department. "We're still sorting out the events of the last few days, but it appears we have all the suspects in hand."

"Were Stefan Draghici and Lockwood Nightingale the men behind the kidnappings and the murders?" A reporter near the front thrust a microphone at Paddington.

"Yes, that has been confirmed through the testimony of Mr. Aleister Crowe, Miss Lydia Crowe and Mr. and Mrs. Michael Graham."

"Who employed Nightingale?"

Paddington held his hands up. "I'm afraid that answer is part of an ongoing investigation."

"Think they'll ever find out?"

Michael turned and smiled at Rohan Wallace. He'd come out of his coma only a few hours ago and appeared to be doing well. Nanny Myrie sat in the chair next to the hospital bed and held her grandson's hand. Her eyes were bright and hopeful.

"That's going to be hard to prove, I'm afraid," Michael told his friend. "Nightingale was a careful man."

"You know what?" Molly stood near the window and peered out at the sea. "I'll bet that whoever hired him is related to someone named in Charles Crowe's logs. Even if we never find a way to prove they were responsible for Nightingale, they're still going to get hit hard in the press when that information goes viral."

Rohan grinned at that. "Can't believe Aleister Crowe isn't fighting you for those logs."

"Oh, Crowe got the original logs back. But not till Michael and I copied the logs and released the information onto the internet."

Michael walked to the tea service. "He can sue us, of course, but in the end it's not going to benefit him much. The only ones to benefit would be the army of barristers he'd have to hire." He shrugged. "All Molly and I would need is one good barrister to keep reminding people of the evil Crowe would be trying to cover up. He'd draw far more attention to what actually happened that way. I think he sees that it would be in his best interest to just cut his losses at this point and accept the fact that his family name is going to get the tarnishing it's deserved for almost two hundred years." He held up his cup. "Would you like tea?"

"Please." Nanny Myrie smiled at him.

"A little, if you don't mind," Rohan said. "Please."

Michael poured two cups and took them over. In the two days since the events at Crowe's Nest and the underground maze, he'd healed up some. His face was scabbed and bruised where he'd been cut and he was still getting around a mite stiffly, but otherwise he figured he'd be right as rain in a short time.

Rohan took his cup. "The sad thing is that Charles Crowe's fortune was found."

"Actually, that's not so bad," Molly said to Rohan. "I just had a meeting with Aleister Crowe last night."

"Against my better judgment." Michael returned to his seat.

Molly joined him and leaned a hip against his shoulder. "I pointed out to Aleister that keeping the fortune would probably prove unwise. Charles Crowe had already left a sour taste in the mouths of most people around Blackpool, and the whiff of—"

"Reeking stench, you mean." Michael grimaced.

"—the slave trade would be hard to overcome." Molly wrapped an arm around him and squeezed but didn't admonish him. "In the end, it's best for all concerned if he just gives it away."

Wide-eyed, Rohan looked at Molly. "You're kidding me."

Michael laughed. "I thought you knew. Molly can be quite persuasive when she wants to."

Molly curtsied unashamedly.

Nanny Myrie applauded. "You've got yourself a fine woman, Michael."

"That, Mrs. Myrie, I already knew." Michael roped his arms around Molly's waist. "She reminds me on a daily basis."

"Oh, quit, you ogre." Molly cuffed him on the head.

"So who's Crowe giving the treasure to?"

"I've set up a charity that will give the wealth back to the affected West African countries. Charles Crowe kept amazingly good notes."

Rohan frowned. "Can you really trust a charity?"

Molly smiled. "You can trust this one. I'm going to be heading it up." She looked at Rohan. "As far as the tribal belongings that were found, those are going to be returned to the countries of origin to be placed in museums where the artifacts can be safely monitored.

Many are fantastic pieces that will help shed light on the history of those cultures."

Rohan lay back more comfortably in the hospital bed. "That's good. That's all I was really after."

"I know, mate." Michael nodded at Nanny Myrie. "Your grandmother explained that."

"What about the gypsy gold, though?"

Molly smiled. "I suppose a case could be made for it if there were documentation—which there isn't. Or if Draghici hung around Blackpool to muddy the water with legal writs. Unfortunately he and his clan escaped from the tunnels before Paddington and his men could catch them. They seem to have disappeared from Blackpool and are now on the run from kidnapping charges. I don't think Blackpool will see him again anytime soon."

Michael set his teacup on a nearby table. "I do have one question."

"Of course."

"The man who was killed after I found him trying to talk to you here in the hospital?"

"I knew him as Dunkirk, but you say his name is Harper?" Rohan nodded and looked troubled.

"It was. How did you get mixed up with him?"

"I met him one night in a tavern. He was part of a construction crew working on the marina overhaul. We got to talking over a few pints, and he let it slip that he was a cracksman."

"Safes?"

"Yes. I was convinced that if I could get into Crowe's Nest, I'd be able to figure out where the artifacts were. Dunkirk—Harper—already knew about Charles Crowe's legendary hoard. I didn't go there hunting for the treasure. I went there looking for the artifacts of my people. Newspaper articles and magazines talked a lot about the personal art collections maintained at Crowe's Nest. Things from all over the world, they said. It was logical that whatever Charles Crowe had taken, he'd probably put it on display somewhere in that house. I figured all I had to do was find one stolen item to prove my case." Rohan shook his head. "Didn't count on running into Aleister Crowe and his gun that night." He took a deep breath. "I think I was just drunk enough and scared."

"So Harper was trying to get information from you regarding the treasure."

"I guess so, mate. But why did Darrow's men kill Harper?"

Michael shrugged. "They were afraid that he would grass on the others and reveal that Nightingale had hired Darrow."

Rohan grimaced. "It's a good thing they didn't think I knew anything."

"You knew enough. If it hadn't been for you, none of this would have come to light."

"Do you think that's true?" Rohan grinned. "All these mysteries lying around the two of you, and you wouldn't have kept poking and prodding till you had the answers?"

Michael and Molly started to disagree.

"Seriously?" Rohan rolled his eyes. "Molly, you've been turning this town upside down and inside out since you've been here. And, Michael? That model in the library had been on your mind since the first day you saw it, and every time a chance arose for you to go poking around, there you went." He smiled at them. "The two of you have noses for trouble and mysteries. You're not going to be able to stay clear of them as long as you're in Blackpool."

Molly glanced at Michael. "Let's hope Inspector Paddington isn't thinking the same thing."

"If he is, we'll be run out of town, love."

"Actually, I've decided I'm through with mysteries. They're too dangerous. Not at all like books and movies."

"My thoughts exactly." Michael was a little disappointed that Molly felt that way, but he wasn't going to dissuade her. They'd surely had enough close calls to last them a lifetime.

Molly walked to the window and peered out, as she'd been doing all morning. "However, I heard an odd story about Glower Lighthouse the other day that made me curious. It's one I haven't heard before."

Despite himself, Michael grew interested immediately. "What story?"

Molly faced him. "Did you know the lighthouse is supposed to be haunted?"

"Most places around here are. That's how Other Syde Tours makes its money."

"But this ghost isn't in their script. Mrs. Peck says one of the lighthouse ghosts steals children's toys. Nothing else. Just children's toys."

Michael rubbed his chin and considered that. "Why?"

"I don't know. Odd, isn't it?"

"Yes…" Michael stretched his legs. "Maybe we could wander over that way after lunch. Take a small look round."

Molly appeared to think about it, but Michael knew she'd already made up her mind. "I'd be willing to. Of course, it wouldn't do to mention any of this to Inspector Paddington."

"He won't hear it from me." Michael crossed his heart with his forefinger.

* * * * *

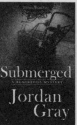

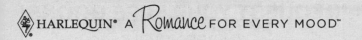

REQUEST YOUR FREE BOOKS!

2 FREE NOVELS
PLUS 2 FREE GIFTS!

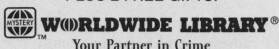

WORLDWIDE LIBRARY®
Your Partner in Crime